MW01230706

PRAISE FOR THE NOVELS OF
KATIE MacALISTER

Memoirs of a Dragon Hunter
"Bursting with the author's trademark zany humor and spicy romance . . . this quick tale will delight paranormal romance fans."—*Publishers Weekly*

Sparks Fly
"Balanced by a well-organized plot and MacAlister's trademark humor."—*Publishers Weekly*

It's All Greek to Me
"A fun and sexy read."—The Season for Romance
"A wonderful lighthearted romantic romp as a kick-butt American Amazon and a hunky Greek find love. Filled with humor, fans will laugh with the zaniness of Harry meets Yacky."—*Midwest Book Review*

Much Ado About Vampires
"A humorous take on the dark and demonic."—*USA Today*
"Once again this author has done a wonderful job. I was sucked into the world of Dark Ones right from the start and was taken on a fantastic ride. This book is full of witty dialogue and great romance, making it one that should not be missed."—Fresh Fiction

The Unbearable Lightness of Dragons
"Had me laughing out loud. . . . This book is full of humor and romance, keeping the reader entertained all the way through . . . a wondrous story full of magic. . . . I cannot wait to see what happens next in the lives of the dragons."—Fresh Fiction

ALSO BY KATIE MACALISTER

MIDNIGHT IN THE GARDEN OF OKAY AND MEH

An Otherworld Adventure

KATIE MACALISTER

FAT CAT BOOKS

ONE
Aisling

"Do you have the condoms?"

"Not on me. I gave them to their intended recipient."

The voices of two women echoed in the bathroom where I stood. I looked up from texting Nora, my former mentor, and greeted them.

"Are we at the condom stage?" I asked Karma and Ysolde, both of whom stopped at the large mirror to cast critical glances at their reflections. "I thought all parties had decided to keep things on the chaste level. Or at least, not full-on sexy times."

Ysolde made a face, an expression that Karma almost identically duplicated.

"I would certainly be happier if Brom waited before jumping into a physical relationship, especially with someone who is only seventeen, but my preferences don't seem to matter to someone of the lofty age of almost nineteen," Ysolde answered.

Karma shot a look at the door before saying, "It took Pixie three entire weeks of hedging around before she came right out and said that she was an adult and wanted to do adult things, and could I please make the appointment with Planned Parenthood that I had offered should she be interested. So now she's protected against unwanted pregnancy, and in possession of a number of condoms that Adam felt was suitable. I will mention the number would have been three figures if I hadn't pointed out to him the message so many condoms was sending."

"Brom has condoms, as well. More importantly, I told him in no uncertain terms that if he doesn't use one, I will personally geld him. Slowly. With a dull spoon. And when he protested that I wouldn't have grandchildren if that were the case, I told him kids were overrated."

I laughed along with Karma at that. "You are the most maternal person I know, so I hope he took heed of the threat."

"I don't know that he would have until Baltic took him out last week for dragon training, and he came back looking suitably twitchy, and asked me to get him another box, since the one we got him last year might have expired." Ysolde, who was wearing her long blond hair in a high ponytail, bared her teeth at the mirror in a lipstick check before hurrying to one of the stalls.

"What on earth did Baltic tell him that could possibly be worse than gelding?" I asked, leaning up against the sink. "The effect of STDs on the human body?"

"Worse. Evidently he went into the hell of a colicky child," came from the stall. "Anduin had colic for what seemed like the entire first year of his life. Baltic estimates he walked near to six hundred miles in the halls of Dauva in order to soothe the baby."

"Dauva?" Karma asked.

"Our home when we're in Latvia," Ysolde answered.

"That sounds like a genuine nightmare," Karma said, tidying her hair. "I'm so glad Pixie was fifteen when I got her."

"It was hell." Ysolde emerged and moved immediately to the sink. "But it was enough to have Brom thinking twice about getting his wick wet."

"Really, Ysolde!" I said with a laugh. "You are such a mix of modern and medieval woman."

"Eh," she said, waving it away as she dried her hands, spinning around to check her skirt wasn't tucked up in her undies. "I made peace with my weirdness a long time ago. I'm just hoping to get through the next decade without going outright insane. Baltic said he'd make me a padded room if that happens, though, and would move in with me, so that's all right."

I laughed again. "Dragons do love better! Oh, sorry, Karma. I'm sure polters are just as protective of their loved ones."

"Eh," she said in an excellent imitation of Ysolde's dismissal. "I'm not saying that they aren't, but it sounds like dragons take it a bit further. I suppose we should go back out there, although I must warn you, Aisling, that we are strictly forbidden to even glance to the right, where the kids are sitting. Pixie swore all sorts of dire repercussions should we monitor how their date goes, and considering how much of a fuss she made about having us in the same restaurant, I'm not going to risk breaking her trust."

"I wondered about them agreeing to us being here." We all had one last check at the mirror, then filed out of the bathroom. Since Bastian's blue dragons—now the Song Tribe—still retained ownership of one of our favorite restaurants in London, Baltic and Ysolde felt it was a safe place for the all-important First Date. "I figured they wouldn't want to be so close since it's six-ties night."

"Evidently, that's part of the plan for the date," Karma informed me, then with studied nonchalance strolled past a small stage that was set up at the far end. Blue booths reminiscent of diners dotted the sides, while in the center, a space had been cleared as a dance floor. "Pixie said Brom suggested they take part in the dance contest, which sounds like a lesser form of hell to me, but to each their own."

Not being one of the affected parents, I took a quick glance at the booth nearest the stage. Brom lounged with one arm resting casually along the top edge of the booth, but his expression was simultaneously suave and terrified.

"Oh lord, I looked," I said, turning my face away so they wouldn't see me giggling.

"At Brom or Pixie?" Karma whispered as we hurried around the corner to the short end of the L shape that made up the restaurant. I noticed she kept her face turned away from the booth in question.

"Brom. He looks in pain."

"Good," Ysolde said with a blitheness that I admired. "That'll mean he's less likely to forget the condoms later."

"I just hope I'm as calm as you are when my kids are old enough to date," I told her as we approached the large round table that was set apart. The men gathered there turned at the sight of us, pulling out chairs for us, their manners impeccable as ever.

"Wine helps," Karma said under her breath, then smiled broadly at Adam, a tall, dark-haired, blue-eyed poltergeist.

"It sure does. Now, there is nothing wrong with that

picture," Ysolde said, flipping her ponytail as she gazed at Baltic, who wore his usual enigmatic expression.

"I mean, I know they're all handsome, but when you get them together in a group like that, hoobah," I said, wiggling my eyebrows a couple of times at Drake, who immediately looked interested, his green eyes flashing at me in a manner that had me suddenly very aware we were going to be separated for a few days while he dealt with some business in Budapest.

"Did you check on them?" Adam asked Ysolde as we all were seated. "Your dragon friend said he'd keep an eye on them for us, but this place looks pretty busy, and he might miss something."

"You have a daughter. You shouldn't be nearly this twitchy over Pixie having her first date," Karma told him, patting him on the arm. He took her hand and rubbed his thumb over her fingers.

"My daughter is in her late twenties, and has a long-term boyfriend." His lips twisted for a few seconds. "I'm not saying I think he's perfect for her, and when she found out I did a background check on him, she gave me hell for weeks for what she referred to as interfering. Pixie, however, is different. She's much younger, and Brom seems a bit …"

"Intelligent?" Ysolde asked, scooting her chair closer to Baltic. "Charming? Handsome, because thankfully he doesn't look in the least like his bio father?"

"All of those things, of course," Adam said. "But he also doesn't seem to be any too steady on his dragon feet, if you know what I mean."

Baltic lost a bit of his enigmatic expression, and donned what I'd come to think of as Drake's martyred look. "He's better than he was. He no longer sets the kitchen on fire trying to feed himself."

"Yes, that's right, he is getting better now that you're showing him the dragon way of things," Ysolde said in the same soothing tone I'd heard her use on her three-year-old son.

Jim, who had been sitting on a flat cushion that Bastian had provided especially for it, reading one of its seemingly endless stash of *Welsh Corgi Fancier* magazines, *tch*ed. "Kid's a menace with his fire. I'm not saying it's his fault, because when the First Daddy bonks you on the head and makes you a dragon, you're going to be extra dragony, but he's still a menace. He set my tail on fire when I went over to see how things were hangin'."

"I explicitly told you not to bother them while I was in the bathroom," I scolded Jim.

"Drake said I could," it protested, then, licking the tip of one toe pad, turned the page of the magazine.

I looked at Drake. The corners of his mouth curled up.

"Bad wyvern," I said, leaning in to kiss the nearest corner.

"Hello, all! How nice to see everyone. Where are … oh, there they are. I assume we shouldn't say hi?" The voice from behind me resolved itself into Allie and her husband, the silver-eyed Christian. They took two of the last four spots at the table. "And what an excellent idea for us to get together now that we're all in London. No May and Gabriel?"

"They're running a smidgen late," I told her, pleased that our new friends were blending in so well with our group.

"Did you bring your kids, Allie?" Ysolde asked, straightening up from where she'd been whispering in Baltic's ear.

"No. They had some school events that they didn't want to miss, so we left them with our friend Joy and her husband and kids. I told Christian we could consider this a romantic getaway." Allie smiled brightly at Christian, who said nothing, but Allie blushed just as if he had.

Ysolde nodded. "It seems great minds work alike. Pavel and Holland are taking care of Anduin while we're in town for a few days."

"We are gloriously kid-free for a few days, as well," I said, putting a hand on Drake's leg, my fingers lighting on fire at the feeling of his thigh just sitting there being so sexy it almost had me fanning myself. "We're renting a place in Scotland while we see if we like the area, so our brood is roaming the Highlands like the wild creatures they are. We're going up at the end of the week after Drake has returned from his business trip to Hungary. So! Here we are, together again, minus the blizzard and imps and fire and Jim peeing hither and yon."

"I only hithered once, and never yonned," Jim muttered, looking up when a server brought menus, water, and two bottles of dragon's blood wine. On his heels were two familiar forms.

"Sorry we're late. You won't believe this, but Magoth is in town, and is insisting he stay with us, saying we owe him for a future act of kindness or some such ridiculousness. Hello, Allie, Christian. Karma, you look well. How is your shoulder, Adam?" May took one of the last two seats, Gabriel settling beside her.

"Much better. I wish polters healed up as fast as you lot, but sadly, it's not one of our talents," Adam answered, flexing his right shoulder, where he'd had surgery a few months before.

"So, elephant in the room," May said after a few minutes of general chat. She craned her head to see around me. "How is the big date going?"

"No doubt just fine. Brom has been dancing to You-Tube videos for the last three weeks in preparation," Ysolde said, accepting a glass of wine. "He said something about winning the dance contest to prove to Pixie that he's worthy, or some such silliness. Honestly, when I was his age, the closest I got to the opposite sex was begging my father's stable boys to let me help them groom the horses."

"You were seventeen when I claimed you from the mortals," Baltic pointed out.

"I was an old seventeen," she told him, smiling at us before sipping at her wine. "Besides, kids aged faster eight hundred years ago. Oooh, an excellent vintage."

"Should we try it?" Allie asked Christian.

"The wine?" He looked like he wanted to wrinkle his nose. I had the feeling that although he appeared relaxed, he was a bit keyed up, but put it down to being amongst dragons. Drake told me that vampires and dragons had always kept each other at a distance. "I don't know that you'd like it."

"It's supposed to be lethal for mortals, but I don't buy that. I drank a full glass before I accepted Drake as my mate," I said, looking at the bottle.

"Same," May said with a little smile at Gabriel that had his silver eyes—which were uncannily similar to Christian's—glittering at her in a wholly approving manner.

"Yes, but you were both a wyvern's mate," Drake pointed out. "And Allie, with all due respect, is not."

Christian seemed to bristle at the implication that Allie wasn't on par with the mates. "She is just as immortal as dragon mates. If she wishes to have some of your wine, I will purchase—"

"It's fine—this evening is on us, since it's because of Brom and Pixie we're here in the first place," Ysolde said, and slid the bottle toward her.

"Will a sip hurt me?" Allie asked Drake.

He hesitated a moment, then shook his head. "No, but I wouldn't recommend you try more until you know how it affects you. I don't think I've ever heard of a Dark One drinking dragon's blood." He looked a question to both Gabriel and Baltic.

"My contact with Dark Ones is limited, so I'm of no help," Gabriel admitted somewhat apologetically to Christian.

We all looked at Baltic.

He stared back at us.

Ysolde nudged him with her elbow.

"Mate," he said in his bossy Baltic tone, "stop poking me in the side. Being a Firstborn does not mean I have in-depth knowledge of all beings in the Otherworld."

"No, but you've been around a lot of places and met a lot of people," she argued.

"Plus, you're kind of … you know … extra," May said. "Your father being a god and all."

"Demigod," Baltic and Jim said at the same time.

Baltic shot a startled glance at Jim, but the latter said nothing, just continued to read its magazine.

"Here goes nothing," Allie said, and, after pouring out about a tablespoon of dragon's blood, raised her glass to her lips.

We all stared expectantly, but none more so than Christian. He looked like he was ready to leap up and fight every person there should Allie react badly to the wine, but I had more faith in her.

She took a sip, had an indescribable expression for a few seconds, then immediately went into a coughing fit that resulted in Christian patting her on the back as she clutched the table.

"Oh, yeah, that first sip is always a lulu," I said, grimacing as she grabbed a napkin and mopped up her running eyes and nose. "Sorry that I forgot to warn you about that. Are you OK? Maybe a little water?"

"I'm all right, just a little … I don't know. Winded? Hoo!" Allie took a couple of sips of water, then shot a glare to the side. Her voice sounded like it was made of rocks. "Although I could do without the 'I told you so' comments."

"Er …" Karma, who was seated next to Christian, looked from him to Allie. "I don't think he said anything."

"Oh, he did," Allie said, coughing a couple more times. Her voice still sounded rough. "You just didn't hear him. Well, I think that quells my curiosity about your fancy dragon wine. Is a normal wine available? I could go for a robust red right about now. One that isn't actively trying to kill me."

Karma and Adam agreed, and an order was put in while the rest of us picked up the menus and considered the options.

"I don't suppose the lamb chops—" Jim started to say.

"No. You heard the vet when he said you can't have chicken, pork, or lamb. Do you want a burger?" I asked.

"Yeah, since you won't let me have the good stuff," it said, nosing over a page of the menu. "But I want extra fries."

"Considering your annual checkup noted that you put on four pounds since last year, your fries will be the standard serving, and no, before you ask, you can't have ice cream. You get way too gassy after dairy."

"Jeez, Ash!" Jim said, kicking the menu aside. "Just embarrass me in front of everyone!"

"My apologies for bringing up the subject," I told the table. "But we've discovered that it's just better if we keep cheese and ice cream away from Jim. Are we ready to order?"

We were, and after placing our orders and reminding the server to make sure nothing poisonous to dogs was put on Jim's burger, we settled in for a chat.

Everything was peaceful until our dinners came, and May turned to Allie and asked, "Did you ever figure out the problem with your thanes? The ones that you thought would turn out to be a threat?"

"Oh, the thanes!" Allie glanced at Christian, whose lips twisted.

"Unfortunately, that problem still besets us," Christian said in a somewhat grudging tone.

"I'm surprised to hear that," Karma said. "Considering how effective you and your nephew were against the imp attack at the airport. I've never seen anyone wield a sword like Finch and you."

One of Christian's shoulders twitched. "Unfortunately, Finch and his Beloved have, inadvertently, made the situation somewhat worse."

"Finch and Tatiana—that's his wife; they met a few months ago and fell hard for each other—now run one of the sections of the underworld." Allie gestured with a fork full of pasta. "We're going to visit them in two months, once they have their area set up. Evidently, even in the afterlife there's a lot of red tape to get things functioning smoothly. The end result, though, is that Finch can't leave his spot without a lot of fuss and bother."

Adam looked more than a little surprised. "Finch is running one of the Hours? The underworld Hours?"

"Yes," Christian said, his jaw working for a few seconds. "It's not ideal, but since he says he is perfectly content to continue the role as lord of the Hour in recognition of his part in the freeing of the thane, then we are happy for him."

"Finch and Tatiana are ridiculously in love," Allie added with a smile at her husband. "When we video chatted last week, they kept making googly eyes at each other. It was so romantic. Although it did drive home the point that it's been ages since Christian googly-eyed me."

"I am a Dark One! I never googled you!" he protested, his brows together.

I gave a mental snicker at the fact that evidently male vampires were just as touchy about things as dragons.

"That term has a different meaning now," Allie told him with a wink, and what I assumed was a grope to his leg, since he gave her a long, slow look in response.

"One of these thanes is out of the underworld?" Baltic asked, immediately capturing my attention. I noticed both Drake and Gabriel giving him the same consideration, mostly due to the fact that Baltic—despite his protestations—had experience with beings that missed the rest of us. He turned to Ysolde. "Did you not tell me that they tried to destroy Abaddon?"

"Yes," she answered, then made a helpless gesture. "But I only know what Allie told us on our 'mates and more' group chat. Why? Is something wrong? I mean, other than the obvious fact that the vampires don't want him out of the underworld?"

Baltic took a big swig of dragon's blood. "If you consider having a formerly imprisoned demigod with vengeance on his mind now released into the mortal world wrong, then yes. It is a problem I would not relish having to deal with." He gave a little nod toward Christian. "You're going to have a hell of a time putting him back."

"I am well aware of that fact," Christian said, and for a moment, he, too, wore Drake's patented martyred expression. I wondered if it was something males learned at some point in their lives, and made a mental note to ask Drake later. "The Moravian Council has been holding nearly daily meetings to discuss our options."

"So far, we have none," Allie said, leaning into Christian. "Finch is researching like crazy from the records in his Hour, but has come up with little more than it is going to take an act of god to get Owain back into the custody of the underworld."

"Oooh," Ysolde said, squaring her shoulders as she set down her fork. "Do I sense a problem needing to be solved by the collective power of mates and friends?"

"A problem!" I said, also sitting up straighter as I exchanged glances with the ladies.

"We can do it," May said, pulling out a small notebook and a pen. "After all, look how well we did with finding Charity for the First Dragon. I'll take notes, shall I? Can we get specific details on this Owain person?"

"I don't think I know what's going on," Karma said, glancing around the table.

"Neither do I, but I think we're about to become a mastermind," Allie said, and pushed her nearly empty plate back. "And I, for one, would welcome any suggestions."

"Beloved, our friends here mean well, but they are not au courant with details of Dark Ones—" Christian protested, but was cut off.

"Yes, but collectively, mates are helpful," Ysolde told him. "And we have a bonus of having the wyverns here, and they know lots of ways to fight people. Baltic's killed many people in a variety of ways, so I'm sure he'd have something helpful to offer—"

"Mate," Baltic said on a long sigh. "As the Dark One says, we have no experience with their kind."

Ysolde held on to a smile as she said, "Which means squat, since they are now our friends, and we are interested in our friends and want to help them. Brainstorm! That's the word I was thinking of. Let's brainstorm some ideas, shall we?"

"If it's anything to do with Abaddon, then you're going to need someone really powerful," May said slowly, her gaze on Gabriel, who, after a moment's thought, nodded.

"Demon-lord sort of powerful," he said.

"Magoth?" I asked them. "I know he isn't a demon lord anymore, but he knows that world better than anyone. Certainly better than me. I was a prince of Abaddon for only a few months."

"Thankfully, Magoth has no powers left. Or near to none." Gabriel continued to look thoughtful. "But there is someone else. …"

"Sally!" May said, nodding, then suddenly frowned. "Oh, but she's mostly powerless, too, now that she's no longer running the Court of Divine Blood."

"That's …" Allie scrunched up her nose.

"The Court is what mortals think of as heaven," Adam said. "My grandmother is the polter ambassador there. The Sovereign is the being—or beings—who run it."

"Gotcha," Allie said, drawing patterns on the tablecloth with a spoon. "And your friend is connected with it?"

"Formerly, and Sally isn't really what you'd call a friend," May said with a wrinkle of her nose.

"She helped us more than you like to admit," Gabriel reminded her.

"Yes, but she also encouraged Magoth to bind me to him, tormented me while I was stuck in Abaddon, and, worst of all, always had the hots for you and was constantly trying to touch you right in front of me," May said with a little growl to her voice.

Gabriel laughed and leaned over to kiss her cheek. "She didn't give a damn about me except insomuch as it angered you whenever she paid me attention. But I do agree that I'm not sure how much of her Sovereign power she retains."

"OK, so scratch Sally," I said, absently watching Jim as it finished its dinner. I'd warned it that it could contribute to the conversation only so long as it was not being offensive or obnoxious, and had something to say that would be of interest to everyone. Its nose was a bit out of joint because of that, and it pretended to ignore me in order to gaze hopefully at May (the weakest against its begging) and the little bit of salmon left on her plate. "If we want powerful, there are two people I can think of. One is Caribbean Battiste, the head of the Guardians' Guild, although … I don't know. Nora—she's my former mentor, and is getting married next month to Drake's guard Pal—Nora says she thinks I could give Caribbean a run for his money. Not that I'd want to, mind you."

"Aisling is a Guardian savant," Drake explained when the polters and vamps looked confused. He didn't look pleased by the fact, but I did hear pride in his voice. "She may have had an unconventional start, but she is quite powerful in her own right."

"Unconventional start," May said, giving Gabriel a cheeky smile. "Like … so badass that some other wyvern tried to steal her."

Gabriel looked momentarily horrified. I laughed. Drake rolled his eyes.

"That is old news, and long forgiven," I told Gabriel, enjoying when he sent Drake and Baltic a pleading look.

"Yes, I think that's best for all," he said, then cleared his throat and added, "I doubt, however—and no offense is intended, Aisling—if even you could deal with a demigod. They are notoriously tricky."

"Ratsbane! I'm going to have to call Dr. Kostich, aren't I?" Ysolde said, her elbows on the table as she dropped her head to her hands. "And he'll make a smart-ass comment about Baltic being fat, and that'll just piss me off, and then we won't end up getting him to help stuff this bad vamp back into the underworld without demanding all sorts of things."

"I could go a long time without seeing Dr. Kostich again," May murmured, but so softly that only Gabriel and I heard her.

"You and me both. Did I tell you about the time he basically started to kill me? I was perhaps a minute away from death. It was in Budapest. I'd say he's a threat to the Otherworld, but he's so damned powerful, I don't know how anyone would ever get rid of him." I leaned back, worrying the problem in my mind. "Maybe if your council sent him a request for help?"

Christian shook his head. "This is an issue to Dark Ones, not the Otherworld as a whole. The Committee would not help us, even assuming they had the power to restore the thane to his prison. No, we must find another way, and while I appreciate the willingness to help, it is a problem for the Moravian Council."

"Not necessarily," Ysolde said, clearly dismissing the vampire's objection. "You don't know how powerful the mates can be when we put our heads together, and you have a bonus of having three wyverns and two polters to add to the collective brainpower. Maybe if we found a way to pressure one of the existing demon lords? Who's the premiere prince now?"

I frowned. "I'm not sure. ... Jim?"

"What?"

I gave it a good, hard look. It wasn't normally surly, so something had to be up with it. "Do you happen to know who the premiere prince is? I know they reset things with the recent renaissance of the Otherworld."

"Paymon." It went back to licking the plate that May had, indeed, set down for it to finish her dinner.

"Maybe if we asked that Sasha person if the Court could help," Ysolde suggested. "The one who told us that Jian was dead."

I leaned down to Jim while May was quickly explaining that Jian had been the red wyvern before his much lamented death, and who Sasha was. "Are you feeling all right?" I asked, unsure if Jim was just being moody, or if something was actually wrong with it.

"Yeah." It was silent for a moment; then it said softly, "It's just that today's my birthday, and no one remembered. Not even you."

"You what?" I said in a volume that had everyone turning to look. "You don't have a birthday. You can't."

"Why can't I?" it asked, giving me a jaded look. "You have one."

"Yes, but I'm human. That is, I was born human." I glanced around the table for support, but everyone looked as confused as I felt. "But you're a demon. Demons are made, not born."

"Yeah, but I wasn't always a demon."

"Oh." I thought for a moment, then patted it on the head. "That's right, you told me you were a sprite before you became a demon. I'm sorry that I didn't realize it is your birthday, Jim. I never thought you had one, or I would have made note of the day, and we would have celebrated. I guess since this is such an important day, I can drop your lactose ban. Would ice cream heal some of the hurt caused by my ignorance?"

"So, you have actual parents?" Ysolde asked when Jim graciously accepted my peace offering. "Human ones?"

"Human?" Jim's face scrunched up, reminding me how amazing I found it that a dog could be so expressive. "I assume they looked human. My mom was from what's now southern India, while my dad was from somewhere in the Balkans. Bulgaria, I think."

I gave a mental headshake to clear my stupefaction. "As fascinating as this is—and Jim, I absolutely want to sit down with you when we get home, and hear all about your parents—we've strayed from the mastermind brainstorming. To recap, we need someone superpowerful. What about the First Dragon? He's very big and bad when he wants to be, and, considering the number of times he resurrected Ysolde and Baltic, clearly has a serious array of powers."

Ysolde had her phone out before I finished speaking, texting someone.

"You're not texting the First Dragon, are you?" May asked, her eyes wide. "That seems … he texts? We could text him? Is he on Instagram?"

"We most certainly *cannot* text the dragon sire," Gabriel said quickly at the same time Drake jerked backward at May's suggestion. "It's not even something I want you contemplating."

May pointed at Ysolde. "She's texting him."

"Ysolde is special," Gabriel said, giving May what I knew he thought was a quelling look, but really was pure adoration with a bit of protectiveness thrown in. "She is the mate of his son. She is accorded rights that are not granted to the rest of the weyr."

"Meh," Ysolde said, still tapping on her phone. "That's not really true, but before anyone gets riled up, I'm not actually texting the First Dragon—to be honest, I'm not sure that he has a cell phone. You'd have to ask Baltic about that, since he seems to have a mysterious way to contact his father that I don't know about. Right now I'm asking Charity if she thinks the First Dragon would be able to help."

"We do not need help from the dragon progenitor," Christian said in almost as much horror as Gabriel. "Much though we appreciate—"

"Charity says she'll ask, but she thinks not. Evidently he's lost one of his kids, and is trying to find out where he is. Oh." Ysolde looked up at Baltic. "She says that Baltic did something with one of his brothers, and now he's missing. I thought all the Firstborn—except you—were dead eons ago?"

"They are." Baltic came perilously close to an eye roll. "They were. The First Dragon demanded I help with the eldest of them. I did as he asked, and brought him to the mortal world, gave him money, and offered to house him in Dauva. He refused all, and left. If that is 'doing something,' then yes, I tried to help him. That is all, and you can stop looking at me like I've murdered someone."

Ysolde returned his annoyed expression. "I'm not looking at you like that. I'm looking at you like you kept the fact from me, your mate, the one who has loved you for the last several hundred years—minus the time my memory was wiped—the mother of your children, and who you claim is your favorite person on earth, and yet you did not bother to tell me you fetched one of your dead brothers from the afterlife?"

"Which afterlife?" Adam asked. "I have friends in most of them, if you need help finding your brother."

"It was a griefscape of his own creation," Baltic said, waving a dismissive hand. "The point is moot. I do not know of Yrian's whereabouts, but I did no harm to him and, thus, am not responsible for him going off on his own. Ysolde, stop glaring at me. There was little to tell you."

"Yrian?" Gabriel said in a voice so strangled, everyone turned to look at him. "Yrian Shadowson? The first of all the Firstborn? The dragon who created the black sept from the chaos of primal dragonkin?"

Drake swore in Magyar under his breath.

Baltic said nothing, his standard inscrutable expression firmly affixed. "I did what the First Dragon asked me to do. What Yrian does is not my responsibility."

"Oh, we are *so* going to have a chat in the car going home," Ysolde told him.

I tried to stifle a giggle, but enough slipped out that May leaned toward me and asked, "What's so funny?"

"Now it's Baltic's turn to wear the martyred expression," I said in a near whisper. "The one that all the men seem to share."

"If we do, it's because we have mates who push us to the limit of our patience," Drake said not very softly.

"That's right, Drake," Ysolde said in a drawling tone that made me give another nearly silent giggle. I knew that tone, and judging by Drake's expression—full-on martyrdom—he did, as well. "But patience has never really been one of your strengths, has it? I seem to recall how impatient you were that time in Prague when we rolled into town for a *sárkány*, and found you in the square about to be hanged for an orgy involving several wives of the town council, and one councilman."

I gave the love of my life a long, long look. "I didn't know you swung both ways."

"I don't," he said quickly, a little wisp of smoke escaping one nostril. "I never have. The man Ysolde and her annoyingly accurate memory is referring to was evidently fluid with regards to gender, not that was recognized hundreds of years ago. And it was *not* an orgy."

"There were eleven women and the mayor. That sounds like an orgy to me," Baltic said as he leaned back in his chair, a glass of dragon's blood in hand. He looked almost happy.

"The whole town was up in arms. They most definitely were going to hang him," Ysolde told the table with what I suspected was great relish. "But then other green dragons arrived and saved the day."

"Ancient memories aside," Drake said hurriedly. I put a hand on his leg again to let him know I supported him, no matter how horn dawg he had been in the past. "It does little to forward the situation. I suspect that what Christian says is true, and that we are out of our depths with a thane."

"We just need someone really powerful," May said. "Anyone have other suggestions?"

"I'm afraid we're less than helpful," Karma said with a glance toward Adam. "Polters are kind of on the low end of the scale, power-wise. Also, does anyone have to go to the restroom? If so, would you take a quick look at what Pixie and Brom are up to?"

I held up my phone. "I had Bastian give me access to the camera facing the stage. You can just see the two of them. They're eating what is apparently enough food for five people."

"That would be Brom's doing," Ysolde said with a little shrug. "Evidently being a new dragon makes you incredibly hungry. Someone powerful ... hmm. Maybe Rowan could help? He's an alchemist."

"He's not going to be able to help," Jim said, licking the last of the birthday vanilla ice cream.

"Who would you suggest?" I asked.

Jim nosed its bowl toward me. "Seconds and I'll tell you."

"How about you tell me and I don't send you to the Akasha for a day," I answered, giving it a look that said a whole lot.

Jim wasn't the least bit cowed. "Yeah, yeah, once a demon lord, always a demon lord."

"Do you know of someone who could help?" May asked.

It rolled onto its back. "Belly scritches? I think better with belly scritches. But use the dragon claws. They get all the itches."

"Avert your eyes, everyone," I said as May, with a little smile at Gabriel, flexed her fingers until they elongated, covered in silver scales, with crimson claws. She scratched Jim's belly and armpits until his back legs were kicking.

"Spill," I told it when she stopped and it flopped on its side with a happy sigh. "Who do you think would help?"

It stood up, shook, and sat back down. "You're just not thinking right, any of you. Ask yourselves who you're trying to capture. This thane is a demigod, right?

One who almost brought down Abaddon. You're gonna need a demigod to catch a demigod."

"We know that," Ysolde said. "We just don't know of one who would work with Christian and his fellow vampires."

"Dark Ones," came a murmur from Christian.

Jim scratched at an ear. "Only the creators of Abaddon were strong enough to stand up to the thanes the first time, so that's what you gotta do now."

I blinked. It was a bad habit when I was befuddled, and I thought I'd gotten the better of it, but here I was, befuddled as hell, and blinking. "You want us to find the founders of Abaddon? One or all of the demon lords?"

"Naw, they weren't around. You need one of the three princes who created Abaddon." It sucked its lip for a moment. "I guess you could ask my dad. Maybe he'd help if he knew it was to stuff the thane back into the underworld."

"Your father? What does your father have to do with anything?" Ysolde asked at the same time May said, "I thought your father was dead?"

"He is. Well …" Jim stood up and shook again. I averted my gaze from the blizzard of black hair that drifted off it onto Bastian's nice parquet floor. "Demigods don't really die—they just kind of fade away. Plus my dad wasn't killed. He was banished to the Lake of Upside-Down Sinners. But that's kind of like being dead, right? It's in the Akasha, after all. The supersecret high-security part of the Akasha. The Thirteenth Hour, the one where they put the bad demigods, and you don't get much badder than one of the three founders of Abaddon. Gotta go walkies. You want to take me, or should I ask the blue dragons if there's a park nearby?"

TWO
Aisling

"I'm not going to say that an actual bomb dropping on the restaurant would have been worse, but *agathos daimon*!" May, who had joined Karma, Ysolde, Allie, and me on another journey to the bathroom, stood next to the sinks and looked as stunned as I felt. "I mean … I can't … Jim's dad is a *demigod*?"

"You know what Baltic muttered under his breath just as we got up from the table?" Ysolde asked, not even bothering to glance at her appearance. She just hoisted herself onto the counter while Karma, with a murmured excuse about too much wine, went to use one of the toilets. "He said, and I quote, 'That explains a lot.' What does it explain, do you think? How Jim found you?"

I paused in the act of washing my hands, startled yet again. "How it found me? I summoned it, not the other way around."

"Mmm, but demigods," May said, running a hand over her glossy black bob. She still retained the appearance of a 1920s flapper, but since the look suited her, no one ever suggested a makeover. "Those are tricky. They can do things that you might not think they could do. What if Jim's dad wanted it to be with you, and made it happen?"

I thought about that for half a minute, shifting to the side so Karma could use the sink that wasn't occupied by Ysolde's hip.

"I don't see how anyone could do that. I mean, I didn't know I was going to summon a demon until that fateful morning, and it was really just the luck of the draw that the summoning caught Jim. It must have been close enough by that when the summon went out, it caught Jim. I can ask it, though. I really want to know more about its dad, because—"

The door was flung open with enough force that it made Ysolde and me jump. Pixie stood in the doorway, her hair twisted into two giant space buns on the top of her head. She was clad in a miniskirt and black lace top, and, since we were in public, wore a glamour to hide her two extra arms. The two that were visible were crossed tightly as she glared at each of us in turn.

"*Deus!*" she all but yelled as she marched into the bathroom, her wrath directed at Karma. "Why can't you trust me? You said you trusted me! I'm seventeen, not a child!"

"And since you aren't a child, I have agreed that you can have unsupervised time with Brom," Karma said with what I imagined was much restraint. I reminded myself that she had been a foster mother for only a year, and sent her a sympathetic look. "Which you have. I'm sorry that the ladies' room is in the same general area as you inhabit, but there's not much we can do about that."

"But they were just in the bathroom," Pixie said, alternately looking indignant and somewhat guilty as she nodded toward Ysolde and me. "You can't possibly have to go again so soon! And why are you all here at the same time?"

"Women always travel to the bathroom in packs," Ysolde murmured.

"It's safer that way," May said, nodding.

"And we usually have things to say to each other that we prefer not to say in front of the men," Allie added.

I pointed at her. "She speaks the way of women."

"OK, but you were just here an hour ago! Do you all have UTIs or something?" Pixie asked.

"Adults," Karma said in the same mild tone that I kept for my kids when they were their most dragon-like, emotionally, "do not comment on the urinary habits of others, especially those significantly older. Although concern for others is commendable, in general, it's best to wait until you know it's appropriate to offer it."

Pixie sputtered for a few seconds before saying, with a few broad hand waves, "Fine! I'm sorry! But it's suspicious when everyone keeps parading past us."

May turned away to fuss with her perfect flapper bob.

Allie coughed a cough that started as a giggle.

Ysolde did the unthinkable. She smiled at Pixie. "All is forgiven, but really, I think you'd better get back out there if you want any of the dinner you ordered. Brom has two hollow legs, and is likely to take your absence as tacit approval of him consuming everything within reach, and possibly one or two dishes that aren't."

To my surprise, Pixie's expression changed from antagonism to humor. She even cracked a small smile when she admitted, "He's been trying so hard to let me have the tofu wings because I said I loved them, but he keeps looking at them as if they are made of gold."

All the dragon mates straightened up at the mention of gold, May giving a little shiver at the word.

"I can reassure you he won't fall over in the throes of starvation if he doesn't eat tofu wings." Ysolde waited until Pixie, with one last pointed look at Karma, left the bathroom before she hopped off the counter and added, "To be honest, I'm surprised Brom even knows what tofu is, since dragons are notoriously carnivorous. Ah well, that's what love—or the teen version of it—does to you. Is everyone finished? I, for one, want to hear more about Jim's father. Do you think he's really still alive? And what on earth is the Lake of Upside-Down Sinners?"

"Beats me," Karma said with a wan smile. "Polters don't mix much with demigods, although I, too, will be very interested to hear about your demon's parents."

When we made it back to the table, I was pleased to see that Drake had returned from taking Jim for its walkies, although the air was now filled with a sort of static intensity. I looked from Drake to Gabriel, Baltic, Adam, then Christian.

"Much though I'd like to say the four of you can have a free-for-all, I doubt if Bastian would appreciate it," Ysolde said, obviously picking up on the same tension.

Baltic instantly looked happy at the thought of one of the bare-knuckle bouts the men occasionally indulged in, the last one having taken place a year ago at the airport where we'd met the vampires and polters. "Teams of two, or one-on-one? We have an odd number. Brom could—"

"Brom is currently wooing the eccentric, but delightful, Pixie," Ysolde told him, sitting down.

"Besides," I said, leaning in to give Drake's leg another fondle. He shot me a look so smoldering, the tips of my fingers lit on fire again. I blew them out one by one while maintaining eye contact. "Bastian would be sure to object."

"Object? To what?" The voice that spoke had an Italian accent I secretly found sexy, although admittedly, it didn't come close to the Hungarian accent that Drake sported. Bastian appeared from the other side of the restaurant, causing the wyverns to all stand in greeting. "No, please sit and enjoy your meal. I'm not staying. Phyllida and her scribe are waiting for me so that we can fly back to Oregon tonight. I thought I'd check in quickly before we return home. Is everything good? From what I could glimpse from the corner of my eyes, the date appeared to be going well. The young lady was speaking most animatedly, while Brom looked suitably starry-eyed. But what is it that I would object to?"

"Fisticuffs," Baltic said with satisfaction, removing his cuff links and suit jacket. "With you here, we can do three teams."

"There is no way Bastian wants anyone fighting in his nice restaurant—" I started to say, but to my horror, Bastian immediately whipped out his phone, tapping madly on it.

"How long will it take? Shall we say half an hour? I will tell Phyllida that I have been delayed a short while," he said while simultaneously trying to roll up the sleeves of his shirt.

"Oh, for Pete's sake. Drake! We are here to help our friends, not beat the tar out of them!" I protested when the love of my life briskly shucked his suit coat, tie, cuff links, and, after a moment's narrowed eyes at Baltic, the signet ring I'd given him for our last anniversary.

"You can't possibly think of fighting here," May told Gabriel, who, like the other wyverns, was divesting himself of constraining clothing and any jewelry that might be damaged. Adam and Christian exchanged glances, then both stood and did the same. "This is a restaurant!"

"We'll go out to the garden," Bastian said. "It's too cold to seat people out there at this time of the year, so we'll have it to ourselves. Drake, shall we?"

"I am not pairing up with Baltic again," Gabriel said abruptly, and nodded toward Christian. "If you would care to be a team?"

"Certainly," Christian agreed, which made Allie roll her eyes.

"I don't suppose there's any chance to stop them?" she asked us.

"Not when they've already started stripping down," Ysolde said, absently picking up Baltic's shirt from where he'd tossed it on the table.

Drake caught me admiring Baltic's famed six-pack. *"Kincsem,"* he said, his fire high.

I smiled and kissed him on the tip of his adorable nose. "Ysolde doesn't mind if I look."

"Certainly not. Baltic's abs are a sight to behold, and I'm happy for others to admire them as I do," she said calmly, sipping at her wine.

"But I *do* mind," Drake told me with a long warning look that made me smile to myself. "How long?"

I made a face, and glanced at Ysolde. "Ten minutes?"

"Twenty," Baltic countered, glaring at Gabriel and cracking his knuckles.

"We will settle on fifteen minutes, with bare fists only. No dragon form, no vampire powers, no polter flickering," Ysolde answered, pulling up a timer on her phone. "And the usual rules about injuries apply—if you get hurt, Gabriel has to fix you up."

"With his magic dragon saliva," May added in obvious enjoyment when all the men looked disgusted, especially Gabriel.

"We have an ointment made from the enzymes in our saliva for a reason," he told her sternly, then ruined the effect by caressing her hair before following Bastian to the tiny garden area behind the restaurant.

Baltic and Adam exchanged glances. "You are bigger than Bastian," the former told the polter. "I like that."

"I'm also a black belt in Tae Kwon Do," Adam said as he flexed his pecs.

I pursed my lips at the sight, not wanting to offend either him or Karma with outright admiration.

"Excellent. We will take the others handily," Baltic said with obvious pleasure.

"I take it there's some animosity between you and the other dragons?" Adam asked as he and Baltic left the room.

"Something like that," drifted back to us as the door to the hallway closed behind them.

"Hoo," Allie said, fanning herself with her napkin before grinning at no one in particular. "I have to say that seeing them all like that is just as effective as it was at Christmas. Do they even make unattractive dragons and polters?"

"Sadly, yes to the latter," Karma said, looking very much like the cat who ate the cream. "Although I will admit that Adam is easy on the eyes."

"Very easy," Ysolde said, then frowned. "Was that out of line, Karma? If you'd prefer we not admire Adam—"

"Oh, I don't mind others looking. I'd kick up a fuss if anyone tried to do more, but I don't think I have to worry about that with you all," she said, looking toward the door. "Er … should we monitor their fight?"

"It's too cold out," Ysolde said, with a wiggle of comfort.

"It's raining," Jim said, coming in from where it had followed the men. "Do you want me to film the fight for you, Ash? I know how you like to watch Drake beat the crap out of Baltic."

Ysolde gave a ladylike snort even as I protested that I did no such thing.

"Baltic can handle Drake," she said. "And he has Adam as extra muscle. I'd rather discuss the situation with Jim's father, but if everyone else wants to go watch—"

We decided as a group that we'd let the men have their fun out in the cold, wet garden. "At least until we take care of the problem with the vamps," May said, pouring out another glass of dragon's blood. "Jim, how long has your father been imprisoned?"

"And just what is the Lake of Upside-Down Sinners?" I asked as it flopped down on the dog bed and once again resumed perusing its magazine. "I've never heard of it. You said it's in part of the Akasha?"

"Do I look like an encyclopedia?" it asked, clearly still a bit offended about the fact that I was ignorant of its birthday.

"Jim," I said with as much patience as I could round up. "You will please answer questions when asked, and yes, that is a direct order."

"Geesh," it said, giving a quick eye roll. "Most people who miss their demon's birthdays are a little more considerate, because they feel bad."

"We will address the subject of your birthday later," I told it firmly. "Please answer the questions asked."

Jim heaved a dramatic sigh. "Fine, but if I have to face Cecile without being able to fill her in on the latest in corgi grooming style, it'll be your fault. My dad was imprisoned right after I was born, according to Zizi's chronicles."

"Zizi?" I asked at the same time Karma said, "When were you born?"

"About 420 CE, and Zizi was the Sovereign after my mom died when I was born," Jim said in a matter-of-fact tone that didn't in the least bit fool me. There was pain in its eyes, a deep pain that had me sitting on the floor next to it in order to stroke its head.

"I'm so sorry, Jim," I said, blinking back a few empathetic tears. "I had no idea about any of this. Your poor mom must have … wait, what?"

"Sovereign?" May asked, her expression startled. "Like Sally sort of Sovereign?"

"Yeah. My mom used to be Sovereign. Didn't I ever tell you?" it asked me.

I stared at it, my brain awhirl. "No! Are you sure? That sounds rude, but … the Sovereign?"

"Well, it's what was written down, so I assume it's true," Jim answered.

"I don't think I know how to process this," Ysolde said, rubbing her forehead. The others there all looked similarly confused. "Jim's dad was a demigod, and its mom was a Sovereign. That's just … I mean, you must be seriously badass with parents like that."

We all looked at Jim. It grinned.

"Right, we're going to add that to the list of things to talk about once we get home," I said, wondering if I'd ever be able to see Jim in the light of a mere demon dog. "Because frankly, I don't think I can deal with it right now."

"I can't help but wonder how a Sovereign came to be acquainted with one of the founders of Abaddon, let alone how they came to have a child," Ysolde said, and the others nodded in response.

"It seems unlikely at best," May added, giving me a look filled with questions. I shook my head at her, just as bewildered as everyone else.

"There is one thing," Allie said after a moment's thought. "If Jim's father was one of the founding princes, he must have been pretty bad."

Jim gave a one-shoulder shrug. "Zizi's notes didn't say anything other than my mom—her name was Parisi—caused all sorts of trouble when it came out she was preggers by Desislav, the most powerful of the three princes who formed Abaddon. Then I was born, and my mother retreated to the Beyond because she had childbed fever and they couldn't stop the bleeding. Later on, Hildegarde became Sovereign, and she told me I had a destiny outside of the Court, so I left. I went to join a friend in Abaddon, but she died, too." Jim's brown eyes considered me for a moment; then it rubbed its head on my leg in a gesture of affection that warmed my heart. I gave it a quick hug, a kiss on its head, and a fondle of the ears.

"I'm sorry," I said again, making a mental note to pay it some extra attention. Clearly, I'd been too caught up with our kids, dragon happenings, and Guardian duties to be attending to Jim as I ought. "That's tragic for everyone involved."

There were sympathetic murmurs from the others, but it was Allie who asked the question about which I was wondering.

"Why was your father banished to this upside-down lake?" she asked, watching as May idly drew Newfies on her notebook page. "Did he do something heinous to your mom? No, that wouldn't make sense. Why would Abaddon be angry at him if he attacked the leader of their opposition?"

"I don't think the Court of Divine Blood is exactly in opposition of Abaddon, is it?" Karma asked, glancing toward the door that led to the garden. "I wish Adam were here. He knows a lot more about the Court than I do, but I thought it was a place that basically did good deeds for others, which is why mortals based their version of heaven on it."

"That's it, I think," I answered, and leaned down to Jim to whisper in its ear, "Would you prefer not to talk about your parents? Or just your dad? I don't want to make you uncomfortable."

"Naw, it's OK. I never met them," it answered, then looked over to Allie. "Hilders said when the other princes found out that my dad took my mom as his mate, they figured he would become too powerful with her at his side, so they got rid of my dad by banishing him to the Thirteenth Hour."

"How horrible," May said, rubbing her arms.

"Truly horrible." Ysolde glanced at my phone when I held it out to her, showing her the camera view of Brom and Pixie dancing with abandon along with a dozen other patrons. We could hear the music in our section of the restaurant, but it wasn't so loud we couldn't converse over it. "Imagine being banished because you were in love."

The others offered agreements, but those were interrupted when a figure appeared in the hall doorway.

Baltic stood with blood dripping from his nose, his hair loose from where it had been tied back, and a long red scratch on one of his biceps. "Mate!"

"What?" Ysolde asked, looking up from my phone.

"You aren't going to watch us fight?" He looked so outraged that I had to stifle a laugh.

"We thought it would be more helpful if we worked out the issue with the bad vampire thane," she told him.

He cocked an eyebrow at her.

"Oh, very well. I never could resist seeing your six-pack in action. Feel free to stay here where it's warm and dry, ladies," she said, grabbing both her phone and Baltic's coat to wrap around herself as she followed him out.

"It's wet out there," May said thoughtfully.

"They're shirtless," Karma added, looking speculatively at the door. "Shirtless and wet, their skin glistening in the light as their muscles flex."

Silence fell for three seconds; then we were all at the door trying to get through it at the same time.

We made it to the garden with less than seemly haste, taking up positions next to Ysolde where she stood under an eave.

"Really?" I asked her when I noticed her filming the men's scrummage.

"I thought it would be fun to have for those moments when Baltic is away," she said with an arch look that had me getting out my own phone.

"Next time, you have to stream it on YouTube," Jim offered as it emerged from the restaurant. "Bet you could monetize this. Ow. That looks like it hurt."

"Drake, was that a tooth or your lip?" I called when Baltic and Adam, having taken offense to Drake's spinning kick that sent Baltic staggering backward, both jumped him. They went down in a tangle of limbs, and when Drake fought his way out, his mouth was bloody.

He paused for a moment, obviously running a tongue around his mouth. He then swore in Zilant, the archaic dragon language, and slammed his fist into Adam's gut before charging toward Baltic.

"Dammit. We've single-handedly funded our dentist's summer home in Nice," I said.

"They will insist on doing this," May said, then shouted, "I saw that, Bastian! It's not very sporting to punch Gabriel when Baltic and Adam are sitting on him. Oh, well done, Gabriel, although I'm not sure biting is within the rules."

We all looked at Ysolde, who gave a barely visible shrug. "I wouldn't want to bite any of them except Baltic, but I don't know that it's strictly out of bounds. Shall we make it so?"

"I think that would be best," Allie said, looking worriedly as it was Christian's turn to be pig-piled upon by Drake and Bastian. "After all, if Christian bites them, they'll really feel it."

"Allie has a good point," Ysolde conceded, and, raising her voice over the London nighttime sounds and rain, yelled, "Biting is hereby forbidden. And before you dragons protest, recall you have a vampire in your midst."

"Dark One," emerged from the pig pile, which then exploded to the side as Christian leaped to his feet.

"Five more minutes," I called, admiring the sight of Drake happily taking on anyone who came within reach.

"You know, the first time they did this, I thought you all were crazy," Allie said.

"I'm so there with you," Karma agreed, then applauded when the team of Adam and Baltic linked arms and mowed down everyone else. Gabriel kicked out and Baltic went down on top of him, obviously knocking the breath out of Gabriel.

"But I'm starting to see the reason behind it," Allie continued, her eyes huge as she followed Christian and Bastian now dancing around each other in the classic pose of boxers. "You have to admit that it rates a hundred on the manly meter."

"It's one of the reasons why we let them beat the crap out of each other," May agreed. "Dragons being so emotionally volatile, it vents their steam, so to speak, and makes them much more reasonable to deal with."

"Little bird!" Gabriel's head popped up out of the writhing mass that was the men trying repeatedly to get to their feet, only to be dragged back down into combat. "We are not unreasonable! Dammit, Drake! Bastian just kicked me there. Two inches higher and I'll reciprocate."

"You boys know the rules. No attacks on any parts we want working hale and hearty. Three minutes," Ysolde told them.

As was usual in these skirmishes, the bond of pairs broke down in the last few minutes, and it was every man for himself. By the time they dragged themselves inside to our table, they were all limping, were covered in wet grass and flecks of mud, and had a generally bedraggled state that did not diminish their inherent sexiness one single iota.

"I think … yes, I think we'll take up your friend's offer of using his office for a few minutes," Allie said, studying a slightly wobbly Christian. "Come along, you valiant vamp, you. Let's get you fed so you can heal up."

"Interesting that feeding fixes vampires hurts," May said as Gabriel plopped down in a chair with a whole lot less grace than was normal.

Drake limped over to hold my chair, but I pushed him gently into his own before dipping a napkin in water to clean up his mouth. "Please tell me it wasn't one of your real teeth that was knocked out. Oh, man. It was. Well, you now have a full house of implants. You're just lucky dragons heal so fast from dental surgery."

"Baltic still has all his original teeth," Ysolde said with zero modesty as she took care of Baltic's gruesomely bleeding ear and face.

Bastian, who had collapsed onto an extra chair he'd dragged over, was sipping at the glass of wine Ysolde had given him. "Not for lack of us trying to make him swallow them. *Peste!* I think one of my fingers is broken. Phyllida will have something to say about that."

"Spoken like a wyvern truly mated," I told him, studying Drake. He was now also sipping at the dragon's blood, and looked more cheerful and less pained.

Bastian's shoulders slumped for a few seconds. "Wyvern no more, but I do not complain. The Song Tribe is stronger than ever, and we hope to do something with the other tribes not under Xavier's influence. A collective like the weyr is what Hunter, Archer, and I are thinking."

"I believe that discussion is best left for a later time," Drake said, not flickering his gaze toward where Karma was wiping up a couple of scratches on Adam's chest before assisting him on with his shirt, but all the dragons present understood.

"I think—phone check, if you please, Aisling, since I don't hear music, and Brom knows full well he's not to leave before telling us—I think we should fill in the men about what we learned while they were out being primal and dangerous."

I was about to open up the link to Bastian's camera, but before I could do so, Brom and Pixie appeared at our end of the restaurant, followed by Allie and Christian, who scooted around them.

"We're going to the movie now," Brom announced, looking simultaneously worried and dewy-eyed.

Pixie, on the other hand, bristled with an indignation that I decided was normal for her. She pinned Karma back with a look and said in a haughty tone, "The movie doesn't end until eleven, so I'm not going to make it back by midnight, because we're going to have fish-and-chips out of a newspaper, and then may go on for drinks afterward."

Adam made an odd checking motion but, after sliding a look toward Karma, sat back and tightened his lips.

"Unfortunately, that is not what we agreed to," Karma said with a collectedness I mentally applauded. "So we will expect you by midnight. Enjoy your movie and authentic fish-and-chips."

"It's legal for me to drink beer here so long as you give me permission, and you have!" Pixie said with a slap of her hands on her legs. "You said I could have a shandy. You can't stop us!"

Karma took a sip of wine before answering. "Do you really want to have this argument right here and now?"

"It's OK," Brom told Pixie, putting his arm around her with a slightly red-faced glance at Ysolde and Baltic. "I told Sullivan I'd be back by then because Mondays are my early-class day."

Pixie, who had frozen when he put his arm around her, slowly turned her head to look at him, her color almost as high as his. "Oh," she said, then started to leave, but evidently remembered her manners, because she paused to gesture toward the table. "Sorry. I didn't mean to make a scene. Dr. Wellbottom says that making a scene when it's not warranted is a sign of lying to yourself. Night."

"Wow," Adam said after they left. He tipped his head as he looked at Karma. "Is that the first time she's apologized?"

"Not to me, no, but it is the first time she's done so in front of other people. Bless Dr. Wellbottom, and may the sun ever rise upon her," Karma answered, still looking a bit stunned.

While the men recovered from their tension-letting, we filled them in with details on what Jim had told us about its parents. Understandably, they were as gobsmacked as we ladies were.

Baltic, I noticed, didn't say much when the other men exclaimed, but he did give Jim a long, long look.

After ten minutes of discussion about how the head of the Court and the head of Abaddon could manage to get together long enough to have a child, we returned to more practical matters.

"What do you know about the place where Jim's dad is imprisoned?" I asked Drake.

"The Thirteenth Hour? I have never heard of it," he answered, rubbing a finger over his chin as he mulled over the information. The rasp of his whiskers against his finger had me considering sliding my hand up his leg again, but I didn't want to tease him to the point where the others might notice. "Is it something you are familiar with, Baltic?"

I expected Baltic to make his usual protestation that just because he was a Firstborn didn't mean he knew everything, but instead, his gaze narrowed on the wall opposite. "Heard of it? Yes. But I did not believe it really existed. It is not something spoken of lightly."

"Do you know if it's possible to summon a person from it?" Gabriel asked, gesturing toward me. "Aisling has summoned beings from the Akasha many times. Perhaps, if this is an extension of that place, she could simply have Jim's father summoned to us?"

Drake's fire immediately roared to life.

"Calm down, sweetie," I whispered to him, giving his hand a squeeze, and smiling to myself when he slid his fingers between mine. Normally, Drake disliked public displays of affection, feeling it was beneath wyvernly dignity or some such silliness, but he was also an incredibly loving man, and frequently emotion got the better of his intentions. "It's not dangerous, but if it were, I'd ask Nora to help me."

"I don't think it works like that." Baltic frowned at the wall, obviously dredging through his substantial memory.

"I have not heard of this Thirteenth Hour, but I must again point out that this problem is one the Moravian Council is dealing with," Christian protested. "I will repeat that we are grateful you wish to help us, but the problem is not yours."

"But if they can help, we'd be foolish to not accept it," Allie told him, her hand on his arm. He took her hand in his, but looked unconvinced. "I mean, you'd take help from a charmer or a Summoner like me, or even a vespillo if it was needed."

"Such individuals could not help us in this situation," he told her. "And naturally, I would accept any help to ensure that our ancestor does no harm to anyone in the mortal realm, but it is a problem best left to those who are experts in the matter."

"Which is us," I said, beaming at him. He didn't look reassured. I turned to Jim. "Can I summon your dad out of the Thirteenth Hour?"

Jim shook its head. "Other parts of the Akasha, yeah. But not that one. I told you it was a super-secure part of the underworld. Guardians can't summon people from there."

"But someone else could?" May said, pouncing on its words. "Could a demon lord do it? If so, we can probably bribe Magoth to do it for us. He'll charge an arm and a leg, because he's materialistic like that, but still, I bet he'd do it."

"If there are any charges to be paid, we will do so," Christian said stiffly.

None of the ladies paid him any mind, although all the wyverns nodded. Adam was talking quietly to Karma, and obviously missed the statement.

"Yes, of course, we'll pay whatever the cost is," Allie agreed. "Just let me know and we'll send the money. Er … is this demon lord trustworthy, do you think?"

"Not so far as you can spit," May said cheerfully. "But he's all we have, so—"

"He's not going to be able to pull my dad out of the Akasha any more than Aisling could," Jim said. I was pleased to see it was no longer flipping through its magazine, and instead was following the conversation with interest. I covertly sent a text to Suzanne, our housekeeper, and asked her to run out and buy a dozen birthday balloons and a box of its favorite dog cookies. "You guys don't seem to get it."

"Then why don't you tell us what, exactly, is needed to free your father?" Drake said in a voice that was as smooth as his massive marble bathtub, but underneath, his fire still simmered.

Jim said nothing, but cocked one furry black eyebrow.

I sighed. "Jim, the order to answer questions did not run out just because we left the room and returned."

"Fine, but if they take away my demon card because I'm giving you information like I'm Google, then you only have yourself to blame," it said with a faux-injured sniff, but I had the feeling that it was secretly happy to discuss the subject. Poor thing, it probably wanted to have a connection with parents it had never had a chance to meet. "The first problem is going to be finding him. He's been in there for sixteen hundred years, so no doubt he's locked away somewhere pretty impenetrable."

"'Find him,'" May wrote on her notepad. "Obviously, that may take some doing. What's the next step, Jim?"

Jim sighed again. "So, my dad, Desi, is a demigod, right? And he's imprisoned in the underworld." We all stared at it until it gave an exaggerated eye roll and asked, "How do you get a dead guy to move around?"

"A hearse?" Karma asked. "No, wait … you mean in the underworld. Adam, didn't you say that your grandfather left your house to go visit one of the Hours of the underworld?"

"Yes," Adam said, looking thoughtful. "We had to hire him a reaper. They're the only ones who can guide the dead."

"Oh, that is not good," Allie said, her eyes on her husband. Christian looked stony-faced in response.

"How so?" Ysolde asked. She was leaning into Baltic, one hand draped over his leg in the same way I wanted to be touching Drake.

"The vamps have a history with the reapers," she answered. "Do you want to tell them, or should I, Christian?"

"No one needs to know about—" He stopped, and heaved a sigh. "No. No! Very well, since you insist, but

I want it noted that I object to baring our laundry, dirty or otherwise, in front of non–Dark Ones."

"Did I just miss something?" Ysolde asked.

Baltic whispered in her ear.

"Really? Mind talking? Why can't you do that?" she asked.

Baltic donned his inscrutable expression again, but his hand must have gone wandering, because Ysolde gave a squeak as she jumped in her chair.

"I'll give you the short and dirty rundown, since Christian is the head of the Moravian Council, and he takes their rules very seriously, but nothing says I have to be quite so reticent to share," Allie said, and we all settled back to listen to this strange (to dragons, anyway) new world. "About fifteen or so years ago, a group that had spent hundreds of years targeting vampires really got going, and were killing vampires in the name of their group. Er …"

"The Brotherhood of the Blessed Light," Christian said with a twist of his lips. "Commonly known as reapers."

"There's a long story involving two vampires named Kristoff and Alec, especially Kristoff's wife, Pia, who was a reaper at one time."

"OK, got it," May said, covering her page with tidy script.

"With her help, and a bunch of vamps, the Brotherhood was basically broken. It tried to carry on for a bit, but we—the vamps—kept at it until the organization collapsed under incompetent leadership."

"Wait—are you saying there are no more reapers?" I asked.

Christian hesitated a few seconds before answering. "There remain a few who were not connected with the

Brotherhood, but they tend to not seek attention, and live solitary lives."

"If there are no reapers left, then how do the dead go on to the afterlife of their choice?" Ysolde asked. "What do they do when they need a guide?"

Allie looked at Christian, who was again a bit reluctant in answering. "According to what Finch told me, I believe the underworlds have automated systems to allow the passage of all but the most powerful beings."

"That doesn't make sense, does it?" Karma asked, looking as puzzled as I felt. "I mean, shouldn't the more powerful beings be the ones who can travel on their own?"

"Yeah, that's not how it works," Jim said. I gave it a pat on the head for offering information instead of me ordering it to do so. "The more powerful beings usually diminish into the Beyond, like my mom did, but if they don't, then they are contained in various Hours."

Silence fell over the table as we all considered this information.

"The answer appears to be simple," I said, my eyes on the notes May had made. "We find one of these reclusive reapers, and he or she goes to fetch Jim's dad from the Thirteenth Hour. I bet even if the reaper person could get him to the regular Akasha, I could summon them both."

"Right, and after we get Jim's dad out, he can help Allie and Christian stuff the bad vampire thane back into Finch's Hour," Ysolde said with obvious satisfaction. "I believe we have a plan, one in which everyone will be happy."

"Far from it," I heard Jim mutter under its breath. Baltic must have also heard it, because he sent a speculative look Jim's way.

"What we need is a Broker to find the reaper," Adam said suddenly. "I can help with locating one, but unfortunately, due to my position with the Watch, I'm not allowed to have anything to do with them. Brokers, not reapers."

"What sort of Broker?" Ysolde asked.

"Real estate or financial?" I frowned in thought. "We can help with both if needed, although I can tell you that Drake is going to be annoyed if we have to barter real estate. You know how dragons are—they hold what is theirs even when they don't show their beloved mates the full listing of their real estate holdings, and she has to find out from a stray comment from Kostya about an apartment in Rio."

"I told you that my mother was living there," Drake answered me with a sardonic twist of one eyebrow. "And you are familiar enough with her to know she'd never willingly pay for her own accommodations when she can use mine. The point is moot, however, since the Broker Adam means is not mortal."

"Broker," Ysolde said, her eyes narrowed on her glass of wine. "Wait … it's coming to me. … Damn my ex for messing up my memories. … Got it! The Midnight Bazaar! That's where the Broker is."

Baltic nodded when she looked for confirmation.

"Show of hands those of us who don't know what this Midnight Bazaar is," I said, suiting action to word. May, Allie, and Karma all raised their hands, as well. "Excellent. Who wants to explain?"

The men all sat silent. Ysolde, with an annoyed *tsk*, said, "I would, but all I remember is that it's located in … Budapest?"

"Amsterdam," Drake corrected, shaking his head. "It was located in Buda until the early seventeen hundreds; then it moved due to the incoming Broker's preference."

"So this person helps you hire reapers?" Karma asked Adam.

"I believe so, although I've never actually visited the bazaar." Adam looked at the other men present. "I assume since the rest of you are much older than me, you have?"

They all nodded.

"OK, so I have added 'go to the bazaar to find the Broker' to our to-do list," May said, flipping a page in her notebook. "I'd like to know a little more about the bazaar. Do they sell magical things there? Is it like the Committee's Buy and Sell group? We've found some fun glamours there, although dragons don't often use them."

No one answered her.

I looked at Drake. "Would you like to do the honors so Ysolde doesn't have to elbow Baltic again?"

"Not in the least, but I will, simply because it is almost the time we told the children we would be home for our video call with them. The bazaar does not market things. … Instead, it facilitates the exchange of services," he answered, once more rubbing a finger over his chin, but this time, I could tell he was watching for me to react to it.

I covertly slid my hand over to his leg, and gave it a pinch.

"What kind of services?" Karma asked.

"Those whose legality is highly questionable, if what I've been told is true," Adam answered before Drake could. "Which is yet another reason why the Watch would be unhappy with me if I were to get involved with them."

"How about I volunteer to contact the bazaar?" I suggested. "Things are light in the Guardian department right now, and we're staying in England and Scotland for the next four months, so I have the time to handle it. I can line us up a reaper to go into the Thirteenth Hour. Jim, if the reaper says it's possible, would you want to go with him or her to find your dad?"

"I guess so," it said, scratching at a spot on its neck.

There was a bit more discussion, but as Drake hustled me off for our video call before he left for Budapest the next morning, we all agreed that we'd go the reaper route to finding Jim's dad.

"I just hope it doesn't somehow end up making things worse," I told Drake as I snuggled against him in the intimate darkness of the car.

"Way to jinx the whole thing, Ash," Jim said from where it had its head hanging out of the window.

"I don't believe in jinxes," I told it, but I could feel from Drake's silence just how concerned he was.

I fervently hoped that Jim wasn't being as prescient as normal.

THREE
Parisi
Winter, Year 420

One of the sprites, Sasha, has recommended that I record the details of my life, since much has happened, and there is much to look forward to in the birth of my child.

My story really begins at a much earlier time. We didn't keep to the tracking of years at that time, but I believe it was close to twenty-eight hundred years before this date, at the end of winter and one of the worse storms I'd seen.

"If I find you hiding ... by the stars and moon, how many rocks look like ewes and lambs? ... I swear by all I know that you'll be made into a stew faster than you can bleat. Aha!"

I stumbled over yet another snow-covered mound, but this one made a feeble noise that was almost whipped away by the wind of the blizzard. Stinging, snow-laden wind burned the part of my face exposed from the cloak of wolfskin I clutched about my shoulders, and froze my fingers when I removed one fur glove to help the struggling form of the two lambs that were curled together under a small snow-laden shrub, their bodies almost frozen.

I pulled the twin lambs out, gave them a quick rub with one edge of my cloak to stimulate their body heat, and tucked them into the mound of furs that lay on top of my wooden sled. A quick search uncovered the corpse of their mother. "Poor thing. Looks like you did what you could to save your babies. I will also do what I can for them, although I make no promises," I told her before returning to the sled to thrust my hands under the furs. It was blissfully warm, so warm it called to me to climb in and take respite from the storm, but my responsibilities couldn't be so easily dismissed.

"Not when people are counting on me to bring back our missing flock. There should be only two more ewes out there," I told the three babies that were gently twitching under the furs. I wove the strongest spell over them that I could manage, half-frozen though I was, hoping it would give them a better chance to survive while I hunted for the missing sheep. "Let's hope the others are nearby. They should be. Ah, that looks like a—ack! What ... what are you? You're not a sheep!"

I had tripped and fallen over something long and, for a horrified moment, thought I'd squashed an innocent lamb, but as I scrambled off the object, the snow was disturbed and I recognized a fur-and-leather-booted foot as belonging to a man. "By the light, I hope you're not—ah. Your chest rises, although slowly. You must not be mortal."

Time seemed to creep by on painful, frozen feet as I worked to uncover the man. Although his face was partially covered by a cloak similar to the one I wore, I could see he had the high cheekbones of men from the Balkans.

"This may not be the most comfortable you've ever been," I said, grunting and gasping through the blasts of wind and snow as I dragged the unconscious man over to the sled. "But at least you'll have the lambs to keep you warm."

The act of shifting the lambs to the side so I could roll the man onto the sled left me breathless and trembling with exhaustion, but at last I had him on his back, with the lambs tucked around him before I covered them all with the furs.

I searched for what seemed like days but, in the end, found only one more ewe, although her lamb didn't fare as well as the others.

By the time I dragged the sled back to the round-houses, the snow was up to my knees, and I couldn't feel anything below my breasts.

"By the grace of the sun and moon, you are back," called one of the cherubs as I staggered to a stop outside the biggest roundhouse, where most of the Court stayed when the weather was severe. The door we'd covered in wool to keep the wind out was flung open, and four people emerged, shivering and moaning about the storm. "What's this? A man?"

The furs had been peeled back as the Court members extracted the lambs and ewes before carrying them into the roundhouse.

"Yes, I found him near where the sheep had gone to lamb." I glanced up at the blistering white sky and gestured at one of the powers who stood next to me, gawking. "Take his feet. We'll carry him in and set him next to the fire."

I ignored the complaints of those who objected to the stranger being brought in, and half dragged, half carried him inside when the power—a man named

Enoch—stood and watched me. I had to weave around the sheep, lambs, goats, and two pigs that resided inside with us, but at last I got the unconscious man settled on a pallet near the fire, and covered him with the furs the others brought in from the sled.

"Well," I said at last, sitting on my heels next to him, panting a little. "We all made it back whole. At least, I hope he's whole. Mags, can you—"

"I'll rub his feet and hands," she said, turning to a group of young cherubs who skulked behind her. "You three put more dung on the fire and warm up some of the nettle stew. My Sovereign, if you would check him for wounds, I'll pack warm stones around his feet and hands."

Despite my own freezing limbs, I scooted closer to the man, and gently, without exposing much of his flesh to the cold, I ran my hands over his neck, chest, arms, and belly. "I don't find any injuries," I told Mags as she wrapped linen around stones used to line the fire pit, and stuffed them under the furs. "Should I check his man parts?"

Mags stopped tucking the furs around his legs and shot me a questioning look. "Do you feel the need to check them?"

"Need?" I shifted uncomfortably, but that was due to my toes starting to come back to life, besetting my feet with what felt like the stings of a hundred bees. "No, not need, but ..."

"He *is* a comely man," she said, nodding. Absently, I brushed a bit of his hair that poked out from under the fur that more or less covered his torso and face. "I can understand you wanting to look, but until his body warms up, he should remain covered."

"That is true," I said, somewhat disappointed, because I had always enjoyed the sight of a fine man part, but knew that Mags was right. She had tended to members of the Court since I had taken over almost thirty-nine hundred moons past. "We will have to assume he's not been wounded there. Has someone warmed a cup of beer? I will see if he will take a few sips."

It took the rest of the day and all of the following before the man finally regained his senses. By then, the storm had subsided, and darkness filled the settlement along with the soft whispers of snow falling from trees and rocks.

I was curled up on my own pallet as night had claimed the land, but hadn't yet fallen asleep when the man spoke.

"You are the headwoman here?"

I rolled over to look into the darkness. The fire in the center of the roundhouse threw out a little light, but all I could see of the stranger was a black shape against a blacker wall.

"I lead all who reside here, yes," I answered softly, slipping out of my pallet to pad over to where he sat against the wall. "You are awake again. You've slept for a day and a half."

"I wasn't asleep the entire time." His voice was smooth as water sliding over polished rocks, making me feel as if my skin were too tight.

"You watched us?" I knelt down, absently reaching for the back of his neck as I had done so often since I had dragged him half-dead from the storm.

"I watched you. You have a curious name."

"Parisi?" I asked, my nose wrinkling, as I'd never been overly fond of it, but my mother said it had been her mother's name, so I kept it. "I was born a great distance from here, where the name is common."

"Parisi?" He sounded almost as if he were tasting the name. "I thought it was Sovereign."

"That's what I am, but not who," I said. "You do not have a fever."

He caught my hand as I withdrew it, spreading my curled fingers until our hands were pressed together, palm to palm. "What is a Sovereign?"

"A leader," I said, trying to see through the dark, but I got only fleeting glimpses of his face when the flames flickered with a swirl of air. "What are you called?"

"I am Desislav, known as Desi. My village is Karanovo, in the Balkans."

"That is a very great distance from here, as well," I said, and told him of the area in the Indus Valley where I was born. "How come you to be so far north?"

The silhouette of his shoulders moved. "Everyone seemed to be going north for the hunting. Like you, I am a leader, and it was decided to create entrances to our domain at ideal locations. What court do you preside over?"

I scooted myself over until I sat next to him on the pallet. The normal nighttime sounds filled the roundhouse along with the occasional tendril of smoke, everything from the snoring of the seneschal to the murmurs of the chickens, goats, and sheep contained in the opposite side of the roundhouse. It was still too cold to leave them outside, as well as those members of the Court who lived in less opulent domiciles. "It is named the Court of Divine Blood. Have you heard of it? We take care of mortal beings."

He jerked to the side, half-turning to face me. "Mortals? You think I am not mortal?"

"Of course you're not," I said, tucking a leg under me and edging one of the skins he'd been using over me. It was still bitterly cold inside the roundhouse despite the sleeping forms of eight other Court members and the dozen or so animals. "No mortal man could survive the storm as you did."

"The storm …" His voice stopped as I saw the shadow of his hand apparently running through his hair. "I remember the snow beginning to fall, but I do not remember a storm. You saved me?"

"Yes."

"Why?" The word contained an interesting mix of curiosity and appreciation.

I thought for a moment. "Because it's what we do. The Court was created to aid those mortal—and immortal—beings who need help."

He gave a short bark of laughter that had a couple of the sleepers mumbling and rolling over.

"What do you find so funny about that?" I asked in a whisper.

"Irony," he answered, then, to my surprise, tried to get to his feet. I jumped up as he wobbled for a few seconds, and held out my hands to steady him. He took them in his, and for a moment, I thought he was simply regaining his balance, but his next words drove that thought out of my head. "When I said I was Desislav of Karanovo, I should have added that I am also the founder and premiere prince of Abaddon, and you, fair Parisi, are now my prisoner."

FOUR
PARTNERS-OF-BADASSES GROUP CHAT

AISLING
Thank you, May, for your comprehensive summary
of the discussion we had last night. I'm so glad you were
taking notes, because it was a bit confusing at times.

YSOLDE
Yes, thank you. Karma, did Pixie say anything about
how the date went? Brom tried to act cool after he came
home, but I swear he just about floated up the stairs. I'm
not looking forward to him finding out that love isn't
always happy songs and steamy kisses.

KARMA
Pixie, on the other hand, was very nonchalant and
all was normal until Adam was out of the room, and
then she got a bit giggly when she told me how Brom
dropped his fish-and-chips down a sewer grate, and
how he bought her a second helping because he said
she was too thin.

I tried to point out that he doesn't have the right
to judge her body, but she dismissed that, because she
told Brom she liked his chest and arms a lot, and if she
could make comments about him, he could do the same

about her. Oy. Being a mom to a seventeen-year-old is much more of a trial than I imagined.

ALLIE

Thank the goddess you have Adam to help. It sounds like he's been through it with his own daughter.

KARMA

He has, and I am truly grateful for him keeping me on an even keel with Pixie. Not that I want to complain, because on the whole, Pixie is a wonderful person. She's bright, and imaginative, and loves to cook, and even helps me with my imps. But the emotions! Lord, the emotions!

YSOLDE

It's running high at our house, too. The emoting! The dramatic statements! The fire everywhere! At least Baltic is on top of dragon training, which Brom sorely needs. Ah, well. It is what it is, and we'll just have to cope as best we can, including turning a blind eye to Brom's overly long, and multiple-times-a-day frequency of, showers. But enough about our young lovers. Is everyone up to speed on Project Thane?

THAISA

Hi, all, from the West Coast of the U.S. I've been following along with the Saga of Brom and Pixie with much delight—and obvious sympathy to the parents involved—but I'm really here because I want to mention our offer of assistance in the whole thane thing. Archer's brother, Hunter, is en route to France, and he said he'd be happy to stop by London and help if he's needed.

AISLING

I'll add him to our list of resources, but I think I can handle getting the reaper lined up, and then it's just a matter of sending her into the super-high-security section. Oh! I forgot to mention that I had a long chat with first Nora, then Caribbean Battiste, the head of the Guardians' Guild, and picked their respective brains about the Thirteenth Hour. CB says it's a fool's errand to try to get anyone out of there, since they had to be "world-catastrophe level of bad" to be put there in the first place. I didn't let Jim hear that, since no one wants to hear their parent was that sort of bad.

MAY

Speaking as someone who has a fairly long history with Jim, I hope I'm not out of line in saying that Jim's dad being the founder of Abaddon just seems to fit, if you know what I mean.

AISLING

Oh, don't worry, Drake and I both see the irony of the situation, but just as Jim isn't truly evil, I have hopes that maybe his dad was misunderstood. Or something.

YSOLDE

I don't think it works that way. Not with demigods, anyway. And this one had to have some dangerous proclivities if he felt what the world needed was a group of powerful demon princes bent on causing chaos and harm to the mortal world.

SOPHEA

I don't know. … Rowan and I are addicted to a YouTube channel that exposes entitled people behaving horribly at grocery stores, and I'm not sure how much better the world is because of them.

SOPHEA

Oh goddess! Now I sound as judgmental as them! Please forget I sent the last message.

AISLING

Don't worry about it. We've all met bad people, both immortal and mortal. So, I think we're set, unless there is any other business re Bad Thane? If so, I have to go see Drake off for his trip to Budapest. He's popped his head into this room three times, and each time he gets a bit smokier around the nostrils.

Karma

I wondered if I was seeing things last Christmas! So, they really do puff smoke?

YSOLDE

Oh, yes. All dragons, male and female, can blow fire and smoke. Baltic doesn't do the latter often because he says it makes his nose tickle, but he will do it unintentionally when he's driven beyond his admittedly thin line of patience. Usually whenever a certain demigod is around.

CHARITY

The First Dragon loves him, too.

AISLING

Hi Charity! Did you have any luck talking to the FD about him popping into this Thirteenth Hour place?

CHARITY

I did speak to him. He just hummed to himself for a few seconds, then said he had a vague memory of the three who started Abaddon, and that he did not feel it was of importance to the dragonkin to interfere.

Knowing that you guys want to help Allie and her vampire, I pointed out that it might not directly benefit dragons, but that it could help the mortal world.

He said it could also harm it in ways no one could conceive, and that his children and the children of the thanes had it within their power to do what was needed.

And then he went off to help his Egyptian god brother with something to do with a prisoner in the Duat.

BEE

What? Is Bael at risk of escaping? Oh man. I'm going to have to tell Constantine, and he's twitchy with weather being nice enough that I take the baby out for walks. If he thinks Bael is about to break out of the Duat, he'll go berserk with worry.

SOPHEA

How is little Winter doing?

BEE

Peachy keen now that she's past a nasty ear infection. But you know how Constantine is—he's convinced that anything outside our home means imminent death for her, so we seldom go anywhere other than walks in the park across the street. But don't let me sidetrack the discussion.

AISLING

OK, that was the fourth and most pointed look from Drake yet, so I'd better hop off. I'll be in contact once I get hold of the Broker. Later, everyone!

FIVE
Parisi

"Your prisoner?" I couldn't help but laugh at the situation, turning my hands so that my fingers slid around Desi's. "I can't imagine anyone who is less a captor than you. I have heard of Abaddon; it is said to be filled with evil, a haven for dark powers and those who would wield them. You are not like them."

A deep, slightly rusty chuckle emerged from him. "Do not mistake my succumbing to a fierce storm for weakness. I am Desislav, leader of the demon princes, and bearer of the blood moon."

Chill swept down my spine, a chill that had nothing to do with the missing wattle in the wooden planks behind me.

As Sovereign, I kept my ears open to happenings in both the mortal and immortal worlds, and I had heard some centuries before of this Abaddon, but other than rumors that three princes ruled strange beings called demons, commanding them to perform heinous acts, I had never come across someone who had actually seen it.

Let alone created it.

"What is this blood moon you speak of?" I asked, smiling to myself when his fingers curled around mine. It was strangely intimate standing with him in that manner, blanketed in darkness, but rather than instill fear in me, Desi was an enjoyable puzzle I very much wanted to explore.

"It is my relic, given to me at birth, the use of which allows me to control Abaddon and the beings in it." His breath touched my face as he stepped forward, releasing my hands to put his hands on my hips.

"Then you are indeed very powerful," I said, giving in to the urging of his hands, and swaying against him, my lips brushing his as I spoke.

"You lead the opposite version of Abaddon," he murmured against my mouth, his lips caressing mine in a manner that stirred my hidden parts. "You must have power of your own. Do you have a relic, too?"

"Sovereigns are made, not born," I told him, sliding my hands up his chest, the rough wool of his outer garments making my fingers feel itchy. I nipped at his bottom lip, giving a little laugh when his fingers tightened on my hips as he jerked backward. "Regardless, yes, I have the strength of my sword arm to keep the Court safe from the mortals, and the powers bestowed upon me to do likewise with those in the Otherworld who would challenge me."

"Including me?" he asked, pressing light kisses along my lips.

It was on the tip of my tongue to tell him that I'd have no problem dealing with him, his relic notwithstanding, but in the back of my mind, a little voice warned that if he could lure me into his arms with just a few words, then I might well be in over my head. "That remains to be seen. Do you wish to bed me?"

He gave another short bark of laughter, and I shushed him, peering through the darkness to where the others lay on their pallets. "You say what you think. I like that. Of course I wish to bed you. From what I have seen, you are lovely. Your hair is as black as squid ink, and flows like the costliest silk. Your skin is warm and enticing, and your body is filled with delightful curves. I am a man. My rod rises for many women."

I stopped kissing the corner of his mouth. "Is that so?"

"It is. But I am very particular in my bedsport partners. I will happily take you."

I slipped backward, eluding his grasp. "Tempting as that offer is, I believe I will pass."

"But …" He moved forward to take my hands again. I allowed him to do so, my sword lying just behind me tucked between my pallet and the wall. "You want me. I can see it in your eyes."

"You can't," I answered with a smile. "Not unless you have exceptional vision. It's too dark to see anything but an outline of your shape. Why were you in this area? Was it to place entrances to your domain near the Court?"

The change of subject took him by surprise, but he didn't answer it. Instead, he pulled me to him again, his mouth hot on mine as his tongue swept into my mouth. He tasted of spices, and heat, and a passion so strong it came close to melting me. I sagged against him again, my hands clutching his shoulders as he thoroughly plundered, probed, and teased me to the point where I started sweating. I took his groan of pleasure and wiggled against him, my body suddenly wide-awake and ready to indulge in as much bedsport as he could handle in his frostbitten state.

"Sovereign? What—gods and goddesses, what is going on?"

I sighed into Desi's mouth, pulled myself (with much reluctance) from him, and turned to face the round shape that stood behind me, having dipped an unlit rush torch into the fire before holding it high so she could see us. "Just as it appears—I am kissing Desi."

"I was under the impression I was kissing you," he said mildly, but there was amusement rich in his voice. It sent another sensual shiver down my back.

Mags—one of the two women who helped me manage the Court, frowned at the mention of his name. "Desi?"

"Desislav of Abaddon," he said, making a lopsided bow. I had to grab him to keep him from tumbling into the fire, but he managed to straighten up without incident. The light from Mags's torch gilded one side of his face, highlighting his cheekbones, long, narrow nose, and blunted chin. My fingers almost itched to touch the short whiskers beginning to show on his jaw.

"Merciful gods!" Mags gasped, then tried to push her way between Desi and me, her arms spread. "Move back, my Sovereign. I shall protect you from this foul one!"

"Mags," I said in as gentle a tone as I could rally given that Desi's chin and jaw and arms and chest held my attention. "Don't be silly. This is the same man we worked so hard over yesterday. He's not evil—"

"I am, a bit," Desi admitted with a half-smile that seemed to do something to my insides.

"—and if he was," I continued with a gimlet glance at the man beside me, "it would be our duty to try to bring him out of the darkness. Is that not so?"

"We serve members of the mortal world," Mags said, glowering at Desi. He just smiled at her in return. I had to stiffen my knees at the sight of the smile, my insides feeling extremely disturbed. So potent was the effect of his smile that I wondered if I might not lose what I'd eaten hours before.

"We also have a responsibility to those in the Otherworld who need our help," I pointed out, the bread in my belly threatening to somersault when Desi took my hand in his. "And if anyone needs help, it is the man who heads up such a foul place."

"It's not foul," Desi said, rubbing his hand over his face. "All right, perhaps it's not as tidy as your compound, and there's an imp problem that, no matter what we throw at it, refuses to go away. And Hath, one of the other two princes, has an addiction to brimstone that tends to make Abaddon smell like a privy that's sat out in the noon sun for many days, but other than that, there's no foulness."

"And the tormented souls you lure to your place of abandonment?" Mags asked, looking like she was ready to strike him. "You do not consider those foul? Of course you do not! You are evil, and thus must be destroyed. Sovereign, I will do thy bidding. Shall I destroy this vermin for you so that the air in our house can return to its untainted sweetness?"

I sniffed. Desi sniffed. In unison, we looked over to where the sheep and pigs were still residing on one side of the roundhouse.

"'Sweet' isn't quite the word I'd use for the air," Desi said with another quirk of his lips.

"Mags, you know full well I don't like to kill beings unless they've done something worthy of such an act, and given that Desi is the founder of Abaddon, I have serious doubts if I could even do so should I want to. Which I don't."

Desi fingered a chain worn around his neck. "You have clarity worthy of one in your position," he told me. "But lest I drive your woman to a fit, I will take my leave of your pristine Court."

"And go where?" I asked when he started looking around for his clothing. We'd stripped all but his undergarments when we tucked him into the pallet, since the stones from the fire and furs had a better chance of warming him. "Mags, do you still have his things?"

"Yes, in a basket, although now I realize we should have burnt then," she said with a curl of her lip. "Not unlike the man himself."

"Ignore her complaints," I told Desi in a low tone when Mags went off to find his garments. "She is very protective of the Court. She was much devoted to the previous Sovereign, and has not looked upon me with copious amounts of favor. Where do you plan on going?"

He gave me a long, long look that made me feel as if I were sunk neck deep in a tub of warm water. "Does it matter?"

"Yes, of course. Evidently, you are my archenemy, and thus I should monitor your comings and goings," I said, a bit breathless under the effect of his eyes and jaw, and—gods and goddesses—that chest. "It's only right and proper that I do so."

He pulled me against him again, his lips whispers on mine as he said, "Will you come with me?"

"To Abaddon?" I asked, both scandalized by the question and intrigued. "As your prisoner?"

"I was thinking more as my consort," he said, his lips burning on mine as I moaned into his mouth.

He took charge of the kiss, the fleeting touches of his tongue building a fire in my nether parts that made me worry a little. Should nether parts feel this hot? I'd been with men before, and although I enjoyed myself, never had anyone inflamed my women's area.

"I am the Sovereign of the Court of Divine Blood," I reminded him. "I doubt if being your consort at the same time is going to work."

He looked thoughtful for a moment. "You're right. I should probably make it a rule that no member of Abaddon can also be a Sovereign."

"Here are your furs and weapons," Mags said as she marched up with one of our storage baskets, dumping the things at his feet before giving him a righteous sniff. "Now you may leave and allow the Sovereign the peace you have so clearly disturbed."

I helped Desi gather his things together, and even assisted in strapping on the various pieces of fur that he wore over his braies and stockings.

"I will see you to the rise to the south," I told him before shooting Mags a look when she started to protest at me accompanying him. "It has an excellent view of the valley. You should be able to get your bearings from there."

"I would be most grateful for your help, and since I can see the words trembling on your serving woman's lips, I will keep myself from abducting you with an eye to seduction, and instead leave you as you are."

It was a near thing, but I managed to keep the words, "But what if I want to be seduced?" behind my teeth, and instead accompanied him out into the frosty morning air.

The sun was just rising, stretching soft peach colors across a lightening sky, the snow that had yet to melt crunching underfoot as I grabbed my sled and gestured toward the south, where my favorite thinking place had the view of the entire valley.

There was little conversation, since it was still cold enough to strip the breath from our lungs, and Desi was obviously not completely recovered. We had to stop twice on the way up to the ridge so he could rest, and when we reached the top, we both sat on the sled to examine the view.

"I was serious, you know," Desi said after a few minutes' silence.

"I know," I said, my eyes on the frosted green and brown of the landscape laid out before us like some sort of a garment stitched of a hundred different pieces of cloth. "I've never had a reaction to a man like I have with you, but that doesn't change the facts."

He nodded slowly before turning to me, taking my hands in his. I *tsk*ed, and peeled off the scraps of linen and wool that I used to protect my hands in the cold, and retook his, his fingers twining with mine in a way that filled my heart with mingled hope and regret.

"It won't work between us, will it?" he asked.

"I'm the Sovereign," I answered, my gaze dropping to our hands. I didn't even feel the cold with him holding them. "You are lord of Abaddon. By rights, one should be trying to kill the other."

"Demigods are not so easy to kill," he said with a wry smile, but there was emotion in his eyes that fit perfectly alongside my own despair. "You could try, but I fear you would be wasting your time. You wouldn't consider leaving the Court?"

"No more than you would leaving Abaddon," I said lightly, feeling as if a cage of ice were slowly being constructed around my heart.

He was silent for a moment, then shook his head. "No. It wouldn't work. Hath and Wat would never tolerate us being together, even if I was to leave the running of Abaddon to them. Not that they could so long as I have the blood moon." He tugged on the chain around his neck and pulled up a red stone pendant, shaped like a crescent moon and scribed with runes the likes of which I'd never seen.

"It's very pretty," I said, my mind troubled with the fact that I truly felt a deep regret that this man was passing out of my life. I'd had dalliances before—I was prone to warm emotions upon first meeting if the recipient took my fancy—but none had come close to seeming so right as had Desi.

"It is a pale imitation of beauty when seen next to you," he said with another of his half smiles.

"Flatterer," I said, pleased with his words nonetheless. "I have seen my face in the scrying bowl, and it has yet to cause men to fall to my feet panting with desire. You, on the other hand, are the handsomest man I have ever seen, and at least three of the maidservants tried to change the warming rocks we used to keep you from freezing, all so they could admire your form."

He gave a little eye roll, then stood, and held out a hand for me. "Come."

"Where?" I asked, slowly getting to my feet and rewrapping my hands before taking the leather thong attached to the sled. "To Abaddon?"

"No. I have my bearings now. I left a camp to the west, near a copse of trees with a frozen stream. It was that I was seeking when I fell afoul of the storm, and must have stumbled in the wrong direction."

It occurred to me that Mags would be very interested to know where Desi had set up camp, since he would do so only if he intended on placing an entrance to Abaddon there, but as with many other thoughts, I kept that back, and instead took his hand and walked with him.

"Why the sled?" he asked at one point, when I *tsk*ed as, for what seemed like the hundredth time, it ran painfully into the backs of my legs.

"To carry things I find. Also, our sheep broke out of their pen a few moons ago, and we're still trying to reclaim them. Some have lambed early, and we were caught by this storm. It is seldom we see snow after the equinox."

He agreed that it was unusual, and kept mostly silent during the walk to his camp. The snow had melted some the previous day, and the pale sunlight gave me hope that the rest would soon dissipate, as well.

I had envisioned a tent made of bent branches and furs, but when we crested a small hill that was crowned with tall oaks, I stopped at the sight of the stone building. It was square with a flat top, like a tomb built for the Old Ones who ruled the earth before the race of man.

"Come in. You can rest for a bit before returning to your compound," he invited, heaving aside a thick door that he'd evidently made by tying together several saplings.

"You'll just seduce me if I do," I told him, moving toward the doorway to peer inside the structure. Instead of a central fireplace, he had built his firepit into one end of the building, and encased it in a tall stone barrier. I couldn't figure out its purpose, and studied it with much attention.

"Perhaps I'll let you seduce me, instead. What intrigues you about my chimney?" he asked, kneeling before the firepit to assemble twigs and some dried bark before striking a flint several times until the twigs and bark began smoking.

"Your what?"

He explained the purpose of the stones that led to an opening in the ceiling. "It keeps most of the smoke out of the house. The wind tends to drive the smoke inside if it is blowing outside, but for the most part, this works well."

"Hmm," I said, peering around it to take mental notes.

"Parisi?"

"Yes?" I answered, narrowing my eyes as I peered up and inside the odd structure. I could see a bit of pale sky through the opening.

"Do you want to engage in bedsport?"

"Yes," I said, before wiping the soot from the stones onto a scrap of linen poking out from a basket of wood. "But I'm not going to, because I'm the Sovereign, and you're ... do you have an official title like Sovereign?"

"I'm just Desislav, bearer of the blood moon, and first prince of Abaddon. I wish to strip you naked and touch you the way you touched me while you thought I was insensible."

Heat rose on my cheeks. "I had to tend you! You were near death, despite the fact that you claim it's hard to kill you."

"Unfortunately, you are correct," he said, sitting down on a raised pallet covered in furs. His lips twisted as he added, "That will teach me for believing that I am immune to being lost in a blizzard. Will you join me in bed?"

"Yes, but just to sit and talk," I said, and sat beside him.

"You fear you won't be able to leave me should we indulge in lovemaking?" he asked with a smile that was full of cockiness.

"Don't be ridiculous." I dismissed the very idea. "More that Mags is likely to have followed us, and if we dally in here, she'll simply burst in at what is sure to be an inconvenient moment. What will you do now?"

His expression, which had been playful, turned serious. "Return to my work at establishing more entrances to Abaddon. It is time for growth, and I must have the pieces in place before that can happen. If I return here at a later time, will you lay with me?"

"Perhaps," I said, putting my hand on his thigh. "It depends on how you answer the next question."

His eyebrows rose as he waited for me to ask it.

"You could be anything you wanted, and you choose to lead an organization bent on causing chaos and strife in the world. Why don't you see the power of aiding instead of obstructing?"

"And how much of your aid would be truly appreciated if people like me didn't exist?" he asked, leaning in to kiss me. "We bring balance to the world, little warrior. Without Abaddon bringing chaos to the world, there would be no need for order."

"But the mortals," I said, my hands on his chest to keep his kiss from landing. "You don't care at all about them."

"I care, but I also know that being bound without hope is intolerable. Between the two of us, we provide both mortal and immortal worlds with choices."

"In an odd, convoluted way, I understand that, but at the same time, the people you harm make my soul weep," I said slowly, wondering why I was so desperate to make him understand my point of view. "What about the jealous mortal who engages you to harm his neighbor's cattle? How do you justify harming an innocent person? You haven't given him a choice at all, merely given preference to the jealous neighbor."

He was silent for a short time, absently taking my hand and stroking the tips of my fingers that poked out of the linen covering them. "You would put the blame for the actions of this person on me, when it was his choice to do so. I am not the agency for evil, Parisi, much though your woman Mags would argue the point. I merely offer choices."

"Why?" I asked again, looking in his pale gray eyes and wondering if I was mistaken in the sincerity and thoughtfulness I saw within.

"Because I know what it's like to have control over your life taken away," he said abruptly, and stood to stack more wood on the fire. "And I will not suffer that for anyone. Bedsport or not? If it's the latter, then I must set out and try to find my demons. They went to the north and west, and were also likely caught in the storm."

"No bedsport now," I said, leaning in with both hands on his leg so I could kiss him the way I'd wanted to ever since I'd uncovered him in the bank of snow. "Nor can there ever be any. It would be wrong on far too many levels."

He smiled under my kiss, his passion warming me despite the knowledge that what my heart wanted was completely impossible.

"Travel safely," I told him as I tore myself away from him, pausing at the doorway. "Stay warm and fare well, for we shall never meet again except on the battlefield."

"I will be back to the area at the next solstice," he called after me.

"I can never be with you again," I said with a righteous sniff that Mags would have loved, then turned back to see him standing in the doorway, one eyebrow cocked.

"See you then," he said with a small smile and admiring look that warmed me from my crown down to my frozen toes.

SIX
Mabel

I don't know what I was expecting when I was ordered to join a video call, but a screen full of dragons wasn't it.

"Er … hello," I said, counting two female dragons, one male, and a Dark One and his Beloved. "I'm Mabel. Is one of you Aisling Grey?"

"That's me," a woman with long, curly hair said. Next to her sat a big black dog who seemed to watch the screen with an intensity that made me slightly uncomfortable. "I'll do the introductions, shall I? Ysolde and Baltic are here to lend their support."

A woman with blond hair waved. In another window, a man sat half-hidden in shadows, making no sign that he was even aware of the video call, but I had the feeling that, like the dog, he was paying close attention.

For some reason, that worried me.

"Also present are Allie and her husband, Christian."

A woman with dark hair also waved, while her vampire gave a nod of acknowledgment.

"And this is Jim, my demon," Aisling finished, gesturing toward the dog.

"Hello to all of you," I said, taken aback by the presence of a demon. I didn't often have call to work with them. "It's a pleasure to meet you, but I feel obligated to point out that although the Broker told you I was available for the guiding of your deceased's spirit, I am, in fact, busy at the moment, and have limited time to do reaper work. It's not my main job, you see."

"That's all right," the blonde named Ysolde said, making a vague gesture of dismissal. "This shouldn't take very long. It's more a retrieval situation than anything else."

"We would like you to bring someone out of the Akasha," Allie said with a glance at her mate. He, like the dragon half in shadows, had said nothing, but I was willing to bet he was thinking a whole lot of things.

Now, that was odd. "Really? I'm sorry, I thought the Broker said you were a Guardian, Aisling. I must have misheard."

"No, I am one," she answered with a flash of a smile. "And yes, I am fully able to summon people out of the Akasha, assuming that's what you were going to ask."

"The problem is that the man we want you to escort out isn't in the normal part of the Akasha," Ysolde said.

She was evidently sitting in a living room, because behind her, a door slammed and a lanky young man stormed through the room, trailing a waist-high blaze of fire behind him.

Ysolde said nothing, but the man in the shadows heaved a sigh, and without warning, his square disappeared off the screen.

"I'm not sure that I'd consider any part of the Aka-sha normal," I said, a sudden worry gripping my gut.

"So very true," Aisling said, nodding. "But in this case, it's definitely ultra-superstrength Akasha."

"The man we want guided out of there is in the Thirteenth Hour," Allie said.

The grip on my insides seemed to be made of steel, and I started shaking my head as soon as she finished speaking. "No, I'm sorry, that's impossible. The Thirteenth Hour is basically a prison."

"If you're worried about getting in there—" Aisling started to say, but I stopped her.

"The problem with the Thirteenth Hour isn't getting in. … It's getting out. That's kind of the whole métier of prisons," I told her, praying they'd accept that fact and move on. I really didn't have time for it, not now when Papi had me by my metaphorical short and curlies, and I was desperate for a way out of what he wanted.

Two more people appeared in the video chat screen, a dark-haired man and a woman who wore a T-shirt with a silhouette of a line of small buildings, with the words *Axegate Walk: The Next Generation* underneath.

"Good afternoon," the man said in what I thought of as a plummy British accent. I realized he was also a vampire, and wondered what on earth two of his kind were doing mingling with dragons. "Our apologies for being late. We have been interviewing stewards, and one of them got away from us."

"Literally," the woman said, giving the man a wry smile. "He ran off to another Hour."

"This is Finch and his wife, Tatiana," Aisling said. "They are the leaders of the Seventh Hour of the un-derworld, and they agreed to join us in brainstorm-ing."

I murmured something polite, and tried to frame a statement about finding another reaper—although there were only three of us in the world at the moment—because I simply didn't have the time or energy to help them, but before I could, Ysolde spoke up.

"I thought the whole point of being a reaper was that you could take people out of one form of afterlife and shepherd them to another," she said with a slight frown. "I don't see how it works if you can't do that for us and the man in question."

Behind her, the lanky young man reappeared and once again stormed a fire path across the room, loudly pronouncing his general unhappiness with the world, but this time he was accompanied by another man, one who I thought was Ysolde's silent watcher. He followed behind, stamping out the fire. I couldn't help but notice he was carrying two swords, and wondered what on earth was going on.

"Mabel?" Ysolde asked, ignoring the commotion behind her when the two men exited the room.

"Sorry," I said, pulling my attention back to where it should be. "Unfortunately, even reapers have limits to our abilities. Under normal circumstances, we can guide spirits from wherever they are to whatever afterlife they wish to visit, but the Thirteenth Hour?" I shook my head. "I don't have that sort of power."

"Who would?" Allie asked.

I hesitated a second before saying on a sigh, "It would have to be someone very powerful. A demigod, for instance. I'm afraid that I'm going to be useless in this situation—"

"But he *is* a demigod," Aisling said.

"I'm afraid that doesn't matter," I said, holding up a hand when both Tatiana and Ysolde started to speak simultaneously. "Even a demigod in the Thirteenth Hour would require someone of his own ilk to help free him."

"And the First Dragon is being stubborn," Ysolde said, looking disappointed.

"Maybe if we talked to this Dr. Kostich that Aisling and Ysolde told us about," Allie said to her husband, who looked momentarily horrified.

"The Committee has little love for the Moravian Council," he answered, his bright silver eyes almost glowing in the dim light of their room. "Even if we would accept such a thing, we have no idea if he has the sort of abilities needed."

"An archimage wouldn't do," I said with another quick shake of my head. "I'm afraid it's a demigod or nothing. That said, I'm very sorry I can't be of help to you."

Aisling *tsk*ed audibly. "Don't be so quick to assume you can't. After the Broker raved about how talented you are, I'm sure you're just the person for us. We'll simply have to get someone else, someone demigod, to kick-start the shebang. Let's see. Who do we know other than the First Dragon?"

"There's the Entity," Finch said slowly. Tatiana thinned her lips. "Two of them are definitely in the demigod or related category, but they've made it very clear that they will not give us help with our problem."

"They said it was out of their purview," Tatiana added with something that sounded remarkably close to a snort. "It was their fault that we ended up blasting ourselves out of the Hour, which meant the thane got out, too, but heaven forfend they should help."

"Heaven forfend?" Allie asked, her lips twitching.

"I've been reading Georgette Heyer while Finch is working on his book," she answered. "But other than the Entity, I'm afraid we've drawn a short stick."

"What about that anime girl … what was her name? … Sasha! What about her?" Ysolde asked.

Silence fell. I badly wanted to click on the Leave Meeting button, but knew that I'd hear from both the head of the Akashic League and the Broker if I severed the connection without permission from the client.

"Oooh, that's a good idea," Aisling said, pulling out her phone. "I think Thaisa gave me her number. I'll shoot her a fast text with the link to this chat."

I said nothing but, mindful of the clock, moved my tablet to the floor, so I could stretch and warm up my muscles.

Ten minutes later, after the discussion in which various persons of power were considered and dismissed, I decided that I'd given the potential clients enough time to escape without censure from my higher-ups, and, pausing in the act of rolling out my leg muscles, shifted the tablet from where it had just caught my head in the camera. "I'm afraid that I'm going to have to—"

"Hello! I can't imagine what you think I can help you with, but yes, of course I remember you dragons. Oh, but I see we have some Dark Ones here, as well. Hi! I'm Sasha. Do you know Thaisa and Archer, too? Are you all planning for a surprise party for them? Is that why this is so secret? I can recommend a chocolate fountain if you are. Also, if you want me to ask a few of my sisters, they'd love to come. Well … Bree would. Clover isn't any too fond of Hunter —they dated for a few months. She's gone off to find herself until another needy dragon hunter comes around. Put me down to bring the chocolate fountain. When is the party?"

I will admit that I stopped rolling out my thigh muscle to gawk at the screen. Unlike many of the leaders of the Court of Divine Blood, Sasha had no qualms revealing her identity, which made it all that much odder when you considered that she was the head of the whole organization. "Er … " I said. "If there is a party, I'm afraid I know nothing about it. And speaking of that, I should be running—"

"Hang on just a few more minutes, please," Aisling said, and asked Sasha, "Would you be willing to help us get a man out of the Thirteenth Hour?"

"Whoa. I didn't expect that," she said, blinking rapidly. "Who are you after?"

Aisling looked to her dog and said softly, "You can speak, but no personal comments."

"Sheesh, Ash, like I am anything but Mr. Suave? Heya, peeps, how they hangin'? Respectively, that is. How come you're on the ground?"

It took me a few seconds to realize it was addressing me. "I'm stretching, and really, I do have to run. I need to be somewhere in seventeen minutes—"

"My dad's name is Desislav," Jim interrupted, obviously answering Sasha.

Her eyes got big. "You're shitting me!"

"Dude," Jim said out of the side of its mouth to Aisling. "The Sovereign swears as bad as you."

"Your father is Desislav the Destroyer?" Sasha, who must have been sitting, shook her head and stood up. "I'm sorry, furry demon, but there's nothing I can do."

"Desislav the Destroyer?" Aisling asked, her voice going up an entire octave. "Your dad is known as *the Destroyer* and you didn't tell us? For the love of Pete, Jim!"

I had to admit, the demon looked as surprised as everyone else.

"I didn't know, but man, that's a pretty cool title," it answered, its expression shifting to speculation. "I

wonder if I inherit that as his official son? Effrijim the
Destroyer has kind of a nice ring to it, don't you think?"

"No, I do not," Aisling almost snapped. "Sasha, the
person in question is Jim's father, and has a history with
the Court. Couldn't you see your way clear to helping
us despite the destroyer business?"

"Not possible, I'm afraid." Sasha wiggled her shoulders. "The Court is more or less in charge of maintaining the security of the Thirteenth Hour. It would cause
endless trouble if I were to interfere. I'm sorry, but I
can't do what you want."

"But … a demigod—or someone of your abilities—should be able to help give our reaper, Mabel,
the oomph she needs to get him out of there," Ysolde
protested.

Sasha shook her head. Her hair was coiled into two
braided blobs on the top of her head, and they wobbled
as she gestured at the camera. "I get it, but honestly, no
demigod in this world is going to help."

"Well … *merde*!" Aisling said with obvious dismay.
"Now what do we do?"

"Would you mind repeating your last sentence,
Sasha?" Christian the vampire asked, leaning forward
slightly.

She gave a half smile. "No demigod here will help
you. I can just about guarantee that."

"No demigod *here*? Here as in Europe?" Aisling
asked.

"Here in the mortal plane, I believe," Christian said
slowly.

"Ooooh," Allie said, now watching her vampire.
"You mean there is someone?"

Sasha leaned so close to her camera that all we
could see was one startlingly bright blue eye and a bit of

the bridge of her nose. "You need someone who doesn't care about living in the mortal world. Someone who is beyond our laws. Someone who has a connection to Desislav."

"Who—" Allie started to add, but Aisling whooped just then.

"Jim's mom! She was also a Sovereign." Aisling turned to her demon. "Jim, didn't you say she was in the Beyond because she was dying after giving birth to you?"

Sasha's eye closed slowly in what I realized was a wink; then her image disappeared off the call, and with that gesture, I knew my goose was not just plucked, but boiled, eaten, and the leftovers made into mounds of goose hash.

"Aw, crap," I said under my breath, and slumped forward over my outstretched legs. "Now I'm done for."

I managed to get off the call five minutes later by swearing I'd fly out to London, where I'd meet up with Aisling and her demon.

"This is beyond a nightmare," I said as I arrived at the Royal Ballet of Beck building, hurrying my way through changing and making it into the mandatory daily class that served as both a refinement tool and a warm-up for the day's activities.

Two hours after, I explained to the ballet master that my ankle injury—which had left me off the performance list the last two months while I recovered—was acting up. "I'll go to PT," I told my boss, Jean-Philippe, a wiry black man of about sixty. "It's been two months since I've danced, so it can just buck up and get with the program."

He looked suitably horrified at my cavalier attitude. "No, no! Gracious me, no, we can't have you trying to rehearse if your injury is not yet healed properly."

"Well … " I said in an exaggerated hesitation. "Dr. Low originally said I should take three months of recovery time, and I've only taken two. Perhaps I should take that last month?"

"Another month … you looked fine this morning, in company class," he said, making me swear mentally because I hadn't held back at the morning's exercise. "Naturally, however, if you feel discomfort with your ankle beyond the norm, you should have more time without rehearsal."

"That sounds very wise," I said, relieved that I had bought myself time. With luck, I could take care of this reaper business for the dragons and vampires, would escape Papi's demands to do whatever heinous thing he was plotting, and could relax for the first time in nine months. "I will let Dr. Low know that I'm off for another month."

"That wouldn't do, no, it wouldn't," he answered, giving a swift shake of his head. "We can't have you off the schedule for that long. You are scheduled to understudy Beatrix's Odette, yes? You can have an additional week for rest and recovery, but assuming you're cleared for rehearsal, we'll need you back on the schedule."

My spirits slumped at the mention of the principal dancer for whom I was understudying the main role in *Swan Lake*. "I understand, naturally, but if I studied performance recordings—"

"Nothing beats good practice," Jean-Philippe said with obvious dismissal. "Do whatever level of activity you and Dr. Low feel is appropriate in class for the next week, and continue your PT regimen."

There was nothing left for me to say, so I left as quickly as I arrived, texted Aisling my flight number and time I'd arrive in London—and accepted her offer to be picked up at the airport—and made it to my flight with a whole two minutes to spare.

It was only when I was in my seat that I allowed myself to relax, and feel guilty at squeezing another week of no-rehearsal from the company. "But unfortunately, my life is not my own," I said under my breath as I leaned against the window and idly watched the waves of the North Sea pass beneath us.

"Really? Then who does it belong to?"

The woman sitting next to me asked the question. I shot her a quick look, noting the short black hair cut in what I thought of as a 1920s style. Beyond her sat a man with his hair pulled into a curly blob on the back of his head.

"Oh great. Dragons," I said, my shoulders slumping. "Don't tell me—Aisling sent you."

"That's right," the woman said with a little laugh. "We thought that since your … er … type of person is so rare, we'd better make sure nothing happened to you on the way to find Jim's mom. I'm May, by the way. This is Gabriel. He's the wyvern of the silver sept."

"We are very grateful that you've agreed to help us. And the Dark Ones," Gabriel said in a lyrical Australian accent. "It no doubt seems strange to you that our two cultures have teamed up to tackle this problem, but the circumstances are what they are, and thus, we find ourselves working together."

"It's not like it won't benefit everyone in the end," May added, leaning toward me to say softly, "Since we need to get the thane off the street where he could potentially harm both mortals and immortals."

"Thane?" I asked, confused.

"Don't worry, that's further down in the plan," May told me.

"Is he dead?" I asked, wondering just how many people I needed to guide.

"Not that I know of. Gabriel?" May turned to her mate.

He looked thoughtful. "I'm not sure. He was in the Hour that Finch manages, but he's also a demigod, and I don't believe those actually die."

"Right now, we need to concentrate on finding Jim's parents and engaging them to help us," May said. "How long have you been … er …" She stopped, obviously hesitant to use my title.

"A reaper? Since I was about fourteen, although my mother wouldn't let me guide anything but pets until I was an adult."

May's eyes opened wide before she exchanged glances with her dragon. "Animals get escorted, too?"

"Of course," I said, wondering if I could squeeze in a quick nap before we landed. Due to Papi's demand to assist him with some impossible scheme, I wasn't getting much time to rest. "If they want to go somewhere else, that is. Mostly, they stay where they are, but a few—those who were taken from the wild, or pets who want to be in familiar surroundings—prefer to go to a different location."

"How sad," May murmured, shifting in her seat.

I thought about that for a few seconds.

"I don't think of it that way. The animals are much happier when we get to their destination, just as are my human clients. Would you think it's rude if I put in my earbuds and listened to music? I didn't get much sleep last night."

"Of course not! You go ahead and take a nap. We won't disturb you," she promised, and she was as good as her word.

It didn't help me sleep, however. I simply leaned against the wall of the airplane with my eyes closed, and allowed free rein to the deranged squirrels I always imagined powering my brain..

How on earth was I going to balance Papi trying to involve me in something he declared was a grand scheme guaranteed to lead to wealth beyond my understanding, the demands of the dance company, and occasional reaper calls?

And when, a tiny, normally silent voice called out, *when do I finally get to put my own wants and desires first, for a change?*

My heart wept for the chaotic mess that was my life, and I fell into an uncomfortable doze contemplating just how hopeless things looked.

SEVEN
Desislav

PERSONAL ACCOUNTING OF DESISLAV, LORD OF ABADDON, DESTROYER OF WORLDS, AND WORSHIPPER AT THE ALTAR OF BEAUTY, GRACE, AND A WICKED SWORD ARM

"She came as I knew she would." Desi stopped, frowned, then looked at the scribe who sat cross-legged on the floor while writing on a piece of papyrus set upon a wooden tray. "That sounds arrogant. I do not wish to sound arrogant where Parisi is concerned. But I knew the connection between us was strong enough to ensure she would be there, and she was."

The scribe murmured something that Desi assumed was reassurance that he didn't sound like an ass when recounting his story.

"For thousands of years we had been meeting every solstice, every equinox at the stone house, snatching for ourselves a few days of solitude and incredibly intense and gratifying bedsport before we had to return to our natural domains. But for this particular solstice some four hundred years ago, I felt Parisi was owed more than a simple stone cottage. Thus, well before solstice, I set twelve of my legions to rebuild the area outside that entrance to Abaddon to reflect the current trend of Roman villas. The area mortals had begun to trade with the Romans, and it wouldn't surprise me if Rome turned its attention to the local tribes, given their abundance of cattle and iron. It makes little difference to me, but I thought Parisi was the type of woman who would enjoy the benefits of a villa."

On the appointed day, Desi stood in the doorway of the chamber he had designated as his own. Three demons scurried about placing furniture, rugs, statuary, and, on a table next to the bed, copious amounts of fruit, cooked meats, and the finest honey. "No, no, Parisi doesn't favor fish. Put the roast pig out for her." He looked around, wanting everything to be perfect. "Is there both ale and wine? Maybe she'd like some goat's milk. I recall her enjoying that. Let us have goat's milk, as well. Wait ... where is the bread? She loves bread!"

One of the demons scurried in at that moment, bearing a massive wooden tray filled with a variety of bready goods.

Desi perused them, rearranged a stack of oatcakes to look more appealing, then nodded to the table. "Put it next to the cheese. The flowers look a bit sparse. Perhaps we need more. Parisi always enjoys the flowers in the fields when we meet at the summer solstice. Whitney!"

The man who served as his steward bustled into the room, bearing an armful of fresh linens. "You bellowed, my maleficent prince?"

"Flowers," Desi said, gesturing toward the few scattered vases of flowering buds. "I need more. Parisi will not be at all impressed if there aren't copious flowers."

"But … there are no other flowers to be found this early in the planting season," the bread-bearing demon said just before his eyes grew wide when he realized he had spoken without permission. He ducked as Whitney, with an oath, reached out to strike him.

"Hold," Desi said, frowning. "You know how I feel about the beating of demons and lesser beings. They are too weak to deserve such punishment."

Whitney made a sour face. "But surely you cannot object to disciplining those who disrespect you? If you don't exert some sort of control over your vast legions, they will take advantage of you. There are times when you must raise your hand."

"I don't consider answering a question I asked as disrespect," he said, glaring at the steward. "Nor do I condone making a scapegoat of the demons in my legions. You know this!"

Whitney mumbled something as he turned away, but Desi wasn't about to excuse that, and demanded, "What did you say?"

"My prince?" Whitney squared his shoulders before turning to face Desi.

"Repeat what you said." Desi pulled the blood moon out from under his tunic and traced the symbols on it.

Whitney's eyes grew wide with fear, but Desi had to give the servant credit—he did not cast himself down and beg for mercy. Instead, he answered, "I said that I know that it has been so ever since you met Lady Parisi."

"That's right. Keep that in mind when you think to please me," Desi said in a silky voice that had the steward backing up several steps, his eyes wary. "You may leave now, and do not return until I summon you."

Whitney bowed low, and shot a fulminating glare at the demon, who was almost prostrate with appreciation as he backed out of the room after Whitney.

Desi turned back to study the bedchamber one more time, desperately wanting it to be perfect for Parisi.

And then suddenly, she was there, looking around her with wide, astonished eyes. "What is all this? Desi, you've built a villa?"

"You're early," he answered, a bit disappointed that she had seen the building without him there to watch her reaction.

"I am? This is …" She stopped and slowly studied the entire chamber as he closed the door behind her, making sure to slide the bolt home. "This is beyond lovely. Oh, Desi. You did this for me?"

She was in his arms as she spoke, and for the first time in three moons, Desi felt like he had breath in his lungs, and blood in his veins. Her scent, that of warm woman, teased him until he felt nigh on bursting in his braies. "Of course I didn't do this for you. Would the head of Abaddon build a villa on the most scenic spot he could find, just to please the head of the Court of Divine Blood? To even suggest such a thing is pure idiocy."

"And I love you for it even more than I loved you the last time, when you surprised me with the Arabian stallion," she answered, adoration and laughter in her face and eyes. Just seeing her again, feeling her body fit so perfectly against his, eased the constant feeling of iron chains across his chest.

"Only when I am with you does my bond with the blood moon become bearable," he murmured into her hair, his ardor growing when she wriggled against him.

Much to his dismay, she stopped her enticing dance against his rod to look up at him, her gaze searching his face. "It still causes you pain? When we met last, you said it had eased, and you were no longer bothered by it."

He didn't like lying to her—in fact, the only time he had was to assure her that the relic's demands on him were minor—but he knew full well he couldn't do so with her in his arms, her breath soft on his face as she all but exuded love and concern.

"I lied," he admitted, falling victim to her beautiful dark eyes, the browns and gold in them flecked with black. He loved how soft emotions made her eyes almost dewy, and once again he felt as if he were sinking into a whirlpool, unable and unwilling to separate himself from her.

"Desi, my love, my infernal one ..." Parisi laughed, giving him a moment's surprise. "After all the years of us being together, have you forgotten who I am?"

He was about to protest when she took his head in her hands and stood on her tiptoes to press a kiss to his forehead. Her lips burned hot on his skin, causing him to involuntarily jerk backward, one hand raised to his head, but at that moment, he realized the constant searing pain that was the blood moon eased until it was barely noticeable. "What did you do?" he asked, rubbing the spot on his forehead she had kissed.

"Placed a boon upon you." She smiled, her eyes dancing with love and laughter. "Sovereigns, as I have repeatedly told you, can do much to ease the life of mortals ... and immortals, even ones so handsome that it almost hurts to gaze upon them."

"I shall worship every morsel of you in profound thanks that you are in my life," he said, moving her back toward the massive bed he had made just for their bed-sporting.

Her smile faded as she bumped against the bed. "Desi … I feel we must talk."

"We always do talk after lovemaking," he said, quickly stripping himself before standing before her, his fingers spread as he tried to work out if the shoulder brooches on her peplos were attached to the undertunic, or if he could simply whip the outer garment off and still allow Parisi to do one of her enticing dances as she disrobed.

"Yes, but this is important. No, do not shy back like I've insulted your manhood, which—" She paused to look between them, where his rod was happily nested against her sublime belly. "—in no way is deserving of censure. Desi, I tire of meeting only for a day or two every equinox and solstice. I want to spend more time with you. I want more than these short moments."

"As do I, my love, my stars and moon and sky above," he said, his hands skimming her body until, somehow, she was as naked as he, her warmth soaking into him in a way that drove his passion higher. "But I cannot leave Abaddon in the hands of the other demon princes."

"Surely, it would run itself—" she protested just as she always did.

"It would, but only so long as the other princes had control of the blood moon, and to give that up would be to spell disaster for us both." He ran a finger along the line of her cheek, down to her jaw, gently brushing his thumb across her luscious lower lip. He loved that lower lip, loved to kiss it, loved to nibble delicately on it, loved to pay it homage until Parisi sighed in pleasure.

"You could make up an excuse to leave Abaddon for a dozen moons," she said, her eyes filled with a mix of hope and sadness. "Take your relic with you so none could harm you. Then, I could do the same with the Court, and we would be together for much of the time. Yes, we would both have to return to our domains now and again, but there's nothing to stop us from taking extended breaks from it so we can live in harmony."

He shook his head, his heart singing a dirge against the cruelty of fate that bound him to a woman he couldn't have. "The others are already suspicious of me, my love. They have been actively trying to gain power over the blood moon, but there is nothing that can master it. As it is, they are resentful of me and reluctant to heed my dictates. To leave them alone for any time is to court disaster."

"I know," she said, slumping against him, her arms around his waist as he held her close, feeling his sorrow mingling with hers.

"We must be grateful for what we have," he said before kissing her with all the passion that flowed through him, but he knew there would be a price to pay for the joy she brought him.

He just hoped he could survive it, because he certainly couldn't live without the only person whom he loved.

EIGHT
May

"What do you think? Will she be able to help?"

I rubbed my arms, feeling a bit chilled due to the damp weather, and considered Aisling's softly asked question. "I don't know. I hope so. I just assumed a reaper would be … you know. Someone who looks like they herd the dead around. Not pretty and feminine, although I realize that sounds highly sexist."

"I know what you mean," Aisling said, nodding. "She doesn't look at all like someone who shepherds dead people, but as we both know, appearances in the Otherworld are often deliberately misleading. I don't think that's the case here, though."

We sat in Aisling's living room, since Gabriel had recently given up the house upon which he'd held a lease, allowing us to shop for something more permanent in the area. Mabel had left the room to take a call, but reappeared in the doorway just as Jim came into the room from another entrance.

"Hey, the reaper chick is here. Hiya! Name's Jim. Well, it's Effrijim, really, but I never liked the whole thing, although now I can ask my mom and dad why they stuck me with it. Whoa. Like … what's wrong with your legs?"

We all looked at Mabel. She was a little taller than me, pretty, with an oval face and dimple indents on each cheek, and waist-length strawberry blond hair, but as I looked at her legs, I could see what it was Jim noticed. She stood with her feet forming an angle of about 160 degrees.

"What about my legs?" Mabel said, looking down at herself. She was clad in black leggings with a wrap top, and I had to admit, her legs were pretty buff looking.

Clearly, she did not skip leg day at the gym.

"They're pointing east–west," Jim said, moseying over to snuffle her in its normal method of greeting.

"That isn't east–west," she answered, then shifted slightly so that her feet were in a straight horizontal line. "This is. It's also first position. I'm a ballet dancer. Hence, I tend to stand like that, since we strive for perfect turnout."

"That would explain you saying you were stretching," Aisling said, gesturing to a chair next to me. "Please make yourself comfy. And how exciting to meet a real ballet dancer. Where do you perform?"

"A small country called Beck. It got swallowed up after World War I, but regained independence about fifteen years ago." Mabel glanced at the clock on a mantel. "I hate to be a pushy reaper, but the sooner we get this done, the sooner I can go back to a wonderful physical therapist who seems to have magic hands when it comes to Achilles injuries."

"Wow. A dancer, huh? Can you do the splits?" Jim asked, giving her feet a second snuffle.

"Yes. Now, what information do you have on"—she pulled out a small notebook—"Parisi. She's in the Beyond?"

"Yeah," Jim answered before anyone else could. "Can I see you do the splits? 'Cause I've always wanted to meet someone who can do it, but dragons are kind of stiff around the hips."

"That is utter rot," Aisling said quickly, giving Jim a quelling look. "You know full well that Drake's hips are as loose as they come. He's an excellent dancer!"

"The reason Gabriel and I are here is to act as your protection in the Beyond," I told Mabel. "I'm a doppelgänger, so naturally I can slip into it as desired. And Gabriel can join me, although not in physical form. We thought it would be better if you had protection. Just in case."

"Like ... when you do the splits, does it hurt?" Jim asked.

"Oh for the love of Pete—don't answer it, Mabel," Aisling said, thinning her lips at the demon.

Mabel heaved a dramatic sigh and, to my utter and complete surprise, stood up only to bend down to touch the ground a couple of times before standing on one leg, her other leg lifted so the toes pointed straight up to the ceiling, effectively doing a standing split. "It hurts if I'm asked to do it without first stretching sufficiently. Happy now?"

"Yeah," it said, giving her a doggy grin. "That's pretty cool. Almost makes me want to try human form again. *Almost*," it added quickly with a sidelong look at Aisling.

"Can we get back to the business at hand?" Mabel asked, still holding her notebook.

"Absolutely," Aisling said. "Jim, I won't order you to silence because we will want input from you, but you are to confine yourself to answering questions or giving information that will help us. Got it?"

"Sheesh," Jim said, slumping against her leg. "You're so bossy while Drake is away."

Gabriel—who had been visiting the bathroom—returned in time to join me in the disbelieving look I gave Jim. It gave us another doggy grin. "Yeah, OK, she's always bossy, but she's more so when the King of Bossiness isn't around. Hilders told me my mom was in the Beyond, and I figured she'd know."

"Hilders being … ?" Mabel asked.

"One of the Sovereigns who came after Jim's mother, apparently," Aisling answered. "Right, let's get down to business and make some solid plans."

"This is the information Sasha sent us regarding one of the former Sovereigns' notes on Parisi," I said as I gave everyone a copy of the report I'd printed out. "You will note the mention that at the time of Parisi's diminishing—when she retreated to the Beyond so her physical body wouldn't die—the Court was located in what is now Bali, having moved there a few hundred years earlier because its denizens were tired of the cold weather of northern Europe. Gabriel has found Bali's entrance point to the Court, luckily, so we have a very good place to start."

"It's located in a resort outside of Denpasar, the capital," he said, giving Mabel a nod. "Has May told you that we will be quite happy to escort you inside the Beyond? While I won't be able to help with anything physically there, May is very adept with her daggers, and will keep you safe should any threat arise."

"There aren't often instances of reapers being attacked, but I have no objection to you coming with me if you think it's important. Bali. There's a portal shop there, I believe," Mabel said, pulling out her phone. "Ah. In Denpasar, as a matter of fact. Good."

Instantly, I felt Gabriel's spirits slump.

"There is a portal shop, but we were thinking of flying," I said, glancing at him. The expression of persecuted dread was evident on his handsome face, so evident that it made me feel like a monster. "But we might have a better solution. Gabriel just bought a jet, since we're taking so many trips between Australia and Europe, and it's fast. Very fast. I can promise that it won't add much time to the plan."

"But a portal is instantaneous, and I have limited time. *Very* limited. I told Aisling that when she booked me," Mabel said with a finality that irked me. I reminded myself she didn't know the ways of dragons, and how being patient would gain more benefits.

"The problem is that dragons don't really portal well," Aisling said slowly, sending Gabriel a sympathetic look. "Something on the atomic level, I believe."

"My mother tells me it's because we dragons had such a chaotic beginning, but I don't believe it was any more traumatic than other beings'." Gabriel made a face that changed into a smile. I melted at the sight of his dimples as I always did. "But naturally, if you are more comfortable with using a portal, then I shall simply park my body somewhere here in England, and travel with you incorporeally."

"Can you do that?" Aisling asked him. "Portal as your ethereal self, that is. I didn't realize that was possible. I mean, you're not physically interacting with the mortal world in that state."

"I can if I'm bound to an object that travels through the portal." He leaned in and kissed the corner of my mouth. "I can't think of a stronger bond than that of a dragon and his mate, so the answer is, yes, if May takes the portal, then I can travel along with her."

"Perfect. You can stay here, Gabriel. We'll park your body in a spare bedroom. Jim, did you get your back-pack ready?"

"Yup. Got everything I'll need in there: my phone, an extra drool bib, my snazzy new collar that has my name in rhinestones—I think my mom will like that—and enough food for two meals, although I don't think that's going to be enough. Maybe I should have some snacks, too, because what if we get in the Beyond and they don't have anything to nom? You know it takes extra care to make this magnificent coat. I should have snacks. I'll tell Suzanne."

"You will do no such thing," Aisling told it. "If for some reason you have to stay longer than twenty-four hours, I'm sure May will find something to feed you."

Jim looked at me with obvious doubt.

I smiled.

"OK, but you should know that when I had to stay with May while you were having the twin spawns, she never once bought me a burger. She made me eat dog food."

"Those who choose the form of a dog must suffer the consequences," I murmured, and thankfully, the conversation progressed without further discussion about the amount of calories that Jim felt was appropriate.

It took us an hour to send out an update to Allie and Christian (who could not visit the Beyond) as well as the others on our chat group, gather up information about traveling from Denpasar to the entrance of the Beyond, and collect a few things that Gabriel thought we might need.

"I feel like an idiot for asking this, but why is it you have to use an entrance for the Beyond?" Aisling asked as we rode in Drake's antique limo to the nearest portal shop. "I've seen May blip into it at will, wherever she is, without having to find an entrance."

"That's because I'm a doppelgänger. I can slip in and out of the shadow world at will. Others, like you and Jim, have to use one of the official entrances." I glanced over to where Mabel sat cross-legged on the seat opposite, watching the London scenery pass by. "I'm not sure about reapers, though."

"We have to use entrances, too." She gave a barely noticeable shrug and continued to look out the window. "We're really nothing more than glorified guides, and don't possess any powers useful beyond locating a needy spirit and taking it where it wants to go."

"We're learning so many things from our new friends," Aisling said, and promptly sent a text, no doubt updating Drake on the situation.

I could feel Gabriel's nearness, but without dipping into the shadow world—known to most everyone else as the Beyond—I couldn't see him.

Twenty minutes later I stood back and watched as first Jim and then Mabel went through the portal.

"Bon voyage," Aisling said, looking cheerful as she gave me a thumbs-up. "I really hope this works for Gabriel."

"It should. Right." I turned to the portal operators, conjoined twins named Sami and Parek, who watched us with obvious amusement. "I'll step into the Beyond just before I go through the portal."

"It's calibrated for you and the dragon to go through together," Parek said with a nod. "Just remember to keep your arms crossed."

"Will do. All right, here we go." I stepped into the shadow world, and was delighted to see the handsomest man in creation leaning against the door. "Oooh, imagine that. There's a silver-eyed gorgeous dragon waiting right here flaunting his sexy self at me."

"It's a good thing I'm incorporeal right now, because I'd be tempted to show you just how much I love you," he answered, waggling his eyebrows in a way that never failed to make me giggly. "Shall we, Little Bird?"

"We shall," I said, and, waiting for a second for Gabriel to merge his spirit with mine, stepped into the twisting, turning miasma that was the portal device.

Exactly two hours and twenty-seven minutes later, we all entered the Beyond through its Bali entrance, and paused to get our bearings.

"Well, this isn't what I expected," Jim said, looking around with a slight curl of its lip. "Like, why is it so grubby?"

I knelt down to touch the powdery gray substance that seemed to coat everything before showing my fingers to Gabriel.

"Scales?" he asked, quickly moving in front of me in a protective gesture.

"Dragon scales," I agreed, wiping the faintly glittery power onto the side of my leg. "But I thought that dragons—Baltic aside, because of his father—couldn't go into the Beyond normally? Why is the whole place covered in dragon scales?"

"Whoa," Jim said, snuffling a door, which swung open to reveal a grimy garden. We'd entered through a small building in the mortal world, which, when viewed in the Beyond, appeared similar, but just off slightly, leaving me with the feeling that none of the angles in the building were square. "There are dragons here? Who?"

"Xavier," Gabriel said in a low tone that sent a little ripple of apprehension down my spine. "Archer and

Hunter told us Xavier had escaped into the Beyond when challenged by them. I dismissed that as a fanciful interpretation of the situation, but now I see I was mistaken. This bodes ill not just for dragonkin, but all immortals if Xavier has impacted the Beyond in this manner."

NINE
Parisi

"I can force them! I'm the Sovereign—I can make them accept you."

"To what purpose?" Desi, shot me a glare I knew was powered by frustration and denial. "We've had this discussion for so many years I've lost track. The blood moon and I are equally part of Abaddon. I can't remove the relic without releasing the magic it contains, and that would spell doom to the mortals and immortals alike."

"Then leave it there," I begged, kneeling on the bed next to where he lay stretched out, naked and sweating after our bedsport. "I know the other princes would try to attack you without the blood moon to keep them in their places, but if you were in the Court, then I could protect you."

"I can't do that, my love." His eyes, the dark gray that could look so icy, were now liquid, like a stream of quicksilver. "You know it. I know it. I wish our lives were different, but they are not."

"If you could leave the other princes control of the blood moon—" I started to say, but he rolled me over so we were lying on our sides facing each other, one of his legs draped over mine.

"Parisi, there is nothing I would not do for you simply to garner one of your smiles, but what you ask is impossible, and not just because Hath and Wat would destroy the Court trying to get at me, but because now there is a new man petitioning to join Abaddon. He's a dragon named Bael, and he has a talisman of power that he has offered to the other princes should they accept him as the fourth demon lord. I have distrusted him from the time he sought to woo me into naming him prince, and denied his request, but over the centuries he has grown more powerful, and I suspect the Fates have already written his future with Abaddon."

"I can protect you," I repeated, hating the despair that I heard in his words. "The Court can protect you from any number of demon princes."

"Without the blood moon, no one can protect me," Desi answered, his body reassuring despite the situation.

Anger rose in me at his answer, anger and fury and, yes, even a little pettiness as I gazed at the man who held my heart. That he wasn't willing to even try drove me to standing on the bed, ignoring my nudity to glare down at him. "Then I see no future for us. I will not be happy with a few stolen days when we could be living together in harmony. This is it, Desi. I am through with you."

I hopped off the bed and started gathering up my garments, yanking my tunic over my head, but I thought I caught the last edge of an eye roll from Desi.

"Do you not think I'm serious?" I asked, my hands on my hips. "We're through. I never want to see you again. I will continue to thrive and be immensely happy in the Court, and you can skulk back to Abaddon with your tail between your legs."

"I understand how you feel, but there is little I can do about the situation without it ending in destruction of one or both of us—" he started to say, but I was tired of the excuses, tired of the heartache.

Tired of the loneliness.

"Then there is nothing else to say." I continued to dress, unable to keep from admiring Desi's thighs and arse when he rose and donned his linen braies. "Since there is no way forward for us to have a future together, there is no reason for us to ever meet again."

"Parisi," he said on a sigh, taking my chin in his hand and tipping my head back so that his gaze met mine. "Always so quick to make a decision. Sweetling, if there was a way we could be together, do you not think I would move the stars and moon itself?"

Tears burned behind my eyes, but I blinked them away. I was the Sovereign, and a Sovereign never cried.

At least not in front of the man who was breaking her heart.

"We have no future together," I said on a whisper, taking the opportunity to admire his face one last time. "I can't keep living like this."

He said nothing for a few moments, then nodded, and released my chin before turning to the window. I wanted to cry out a protest but gritted my teeth against the words. "You are right, of course. I want more than anything for you to live in happiness and love, so it is only right that you forget me, and fill your life with others who you love."

The wounds struck me like silver-tipped barbs. "Even if it means taking a lover with whom I can spend my life?"

His shoulders jerked, but he didn't turn around to face me. "If that is what would make you happy, then yes."

My sorrow burned hot, and turned into a fury unlike anything I remember feeling. "So you're not willing to fight for us? For what we have? You truly are not the man I thought you were. You're weak, and a coward, and I swear to all the gods and goddesses that I will forget you as soon as possible."

"Live in peace," was all he said, his head bowed as he put a hand against the wall as if to brace himself.

I blinked back even more hot, burning tears and stormed off to return to my own domain, where people behaved in a manner that made sense.

"I will forget him," I growled to myself as I entered the brand-new portal in Bali we'd built to access the Court. "He's nothing to me. Just a very handsome, insanely annoying man, and I refuse to have him in my life any longer."

I sobbed for a week straight.

TEN
May

"I've never seen the Beyond like this," Mabel said, her expression one of stark disbelief as she followed Jim into the dusty garden. "It's like it's been blighted somehow."

"Blight is a very good word for this," Gabriel said as we examined the surroundings. "The Beyond is supposed to be a haven, a slightly altered version of the mortal world where immortal beings can reside in peace. This is no haven."

"It most certainly isn't," Mabel said, then tugged at a necklace of extremely fine silver. At the end was a small crescent-shaped medallion with a milky stone on one tip. Mabel lifted the moon and seemed to study it before looking up and to the right. "I believe the spirit you are seeking is this way."

We all followed her, the excitement of helping Jim meet his mother—even if it was for an ulterior motive—waning as we saw what havoc had been wreaked upon the shadow world. "It's almost as if it's dead," I whispered to Gabriel when I scrambled over a bit of fallen masonry. The buildings here—while representing similar ones in the real world—were in profound stages of decay, with some of them having tumbled down into dusty, empty streets. "It's so quiet, too."

"Please tell me this isn't normal, 'cause otherwise I don't want to go here when it's time for me to diminish," Jim said. Even it was unusually subdued, as if the place was depressing its spirits. It certainly did mine.

"Do demons normally diminish?" I couldn't help but ask.

"Naw, but I'm demon extra plus with whiter whites and brighter colors. Wow. This place really sucks. Is that imp dead?"

"Yup," Mabel said as she skirted a small gray blob. "OK, I think we're coming up on your mother's spirit. Let's see if she's in this building."

We had stopped in front of what reminded me of a Spanish colonial wharf, minus color, water, and any living beings. Mabel consulted her pendant again, then turned and walked to the small cottage half-hidden behind the wharf building. As we moved out from the cover of the building, I noticed a faintly rhythmic sound that I had assumed was the wind rattling a shutter or something of that ilk, but the sight that met us was just about the last thing I expected to see.

A woman stood in what was probably once a quite pretty garden, but instead of rounded bushes dotted with flowers and greenery, mounds of dusty gray powder hid everything but vague shapes. A stand made of wood and bales of hay stood nestled up against a side fence, with a vaguely human-shaped blob hanging from a crossbeam. It was obviously made of some sort of sacking and most likely filled with straw. But it was the woman who had us all stopping as if by agreement.

"Wow," Jim said, its eyes big. "Is that my mom? She's … she's …"

"Seriously badass," I said, watching as the woman danced around the sack figure, a massive, bright silver sword in both hands as she hacked at the target. She appeared to be taller than me, with a solid—but very graceful—figure. Her long black hair whipped around her as she swung the sword. Braids entwined with pale blue ribbons hung alongside her face, reminding me of depictions of war braids.

"She's got armor on," Jim said, its voice filled with wonder and some emotion I had a hard time identifying. Yearning, I thought, but I wasn't certain. "Full metal armor. Where's my phone? I gotta get some video of this to show Ash. She's going to crap over the fact that my mom is a warrior."

"Definitely a warrior," I agreed as the woman stopped fighting, wiping one hand across her forehead before noticing us outside her fence. I dropped my voice so just Gabriel could hear. "Do you think she's dangerous?"

"To us?" He was silent for a few seconds, watching as Parisi—as I assumed it was—strode toward us. A swath of blue was spread across her eyes. "I don't believe so. Is that woad?"

"That's just what I was wondering. … Er … hello!"

Gabriel and I moved forward when Parisi, speaking in a language I didn't recognize at all, marched up to the gate and waggled her sword at us.

"Parisi of Madurai?" Mabel held up her pendant. "I am Mabel, a reaper who has been tasked to locate you."

The woman slowly lowered her sword. "Yes, I am Parisi. A reaper? Why do you seek me out? I am already in the Beyond." Her voice held a soft Indian accent, but the tone was all business. Her gaze flickered through us. "And why have you brought a demon and two dragons with you?"

"That's a bit of a story, and since it's not mine to tell, I will yield the floor to Jim and May and Gabriel," Mabel answered, gesturing toward us. "However, I will remind everyone that I am on a very strict time limit, so any help toward wrapping things up would be much appreciated."

Gabriel sent her a little frown before bowing to Parisi. "I am Gabriel Tauhou, wyvern of the silver dragons, and this is my mate, May Northcott. The demon is a friend of ours. Its name is Jim."

"Hi," Jim said, its expression somewhat frozen. "Name's really Effrijim."

We all waited to see what Parisi would do with that bit of news, but she simply continued to look mildly annoyed. "I would say it's a pleasure to meet you all, but as you can see, I'm very busy training right now. Perhaps if you came back later, say a year or two, then we can have a chat. But right now, I must adhere to my training program, or all my progress will be lost."

"Oh, I hear you on that," Mabel said, grimacing as she wiggled her shoulders. "My body just doesn't feel right if I don't stick to my exercise program."

Parisi pointed the sword at Mabel. "You understand. Are you a defender, too?"

"Ballet dancer," she answered. "Who do you defend, if you don't mind me asking?"

"Those in need. I am a Defender of the Blood. It is my sworn duty to answer the call of those who need my aid. Now, I really must get back to working on my slashing. It's always a useful attack, and one underrated by those who believe stabbing is the way to go. Don Diego, for instance, is extremely wrong about his system of maiming and beheading."

"Who's Don Diego when he's at home?" Jim asked before I could offer the explanation we'd decided would be the easiest to describe the situation.

"My archnemesis!" Parisi said with an audible outraged snort, before spinning on her heel and striding through her garden to her target dummy. "And a damned fool idiot if he thinks I won't take him down if he tries touching my arse again."

I looked at Gabriel, worried.

He evidently felt the same.

"A defender is exactly the type of person we need. We would very much like to talk to you about a problem that we believe you can help with. Would you come with us so that we can have that discussion? I can assure you that Mabel will be happy to bring you back afterward, if that is what you desire," Gabriel said, his voice extremely smooth and persuasive.

"I couldn't leave the Beyond," Parisi insisted, evidently immune to Gabriel's charms, because she returned to hacking up the target dummy.

"Because of who you used to be?" I asked, wondering how we could persuade her if she didn't want to help us. I had assumed that once she saw Jim, she would be willing to do what was needed, but if she didn't accept him ...

"Who I used to be? I don't know who you think I am, but my life is simple: I am a warrior, first and foremost," she insisted, her breath coming short as she worked over the dummy. Bits of straw and shredded cloth drifted in a halo around her. "I protect those who need protecting, and give aid to the worthy."

We drew together and held a quiet conference.

"Why doesn't she know who she is?" I asked Mabel. "You'd think someone who is as powerful as the Sovereign would have her wits together."

"I don't think it's a matter of wits," Gabriel said slowly, watching Parisi with speculation rife in his beautiful eyes.

"It's not. At least, I don't think it is, not being personally acquainted with her. The thing about the Beyond is that the longer you reside here, the more your ties to the mortal realm are severed," Mabel said, nodding toward Parisi. "I think of it as a bunch of tiny threads that start in the mortal realm. The longer someone remains outside that world, the weaker the ties, until they crumble away to nothing. In short, the previous life outside the Beyond ceases to have meaning."

"So she's not going to know who I am if I tell her?" Jim asked. There was pain in its voice, enough that I felt compelled to give it a reassuring pet on the head. Aisling had asked me to take care of Jim, since we were both worried about its reactions to meeting its parents.

Mabel gave a half-hearted shrug. "I'm afraid it's likely she won't, but I could be wrong."

"What happens if she returns to the mortal world?" Gabriel asked. "Would those ties that were severed reform? Or are her memories of the past gone?"

"That I can't tell you," Mabel answered, sliding a glance at her phone. "Also, my time for this job is almost over. Is there something else I can do for you?"

"I'm not going to just go away without seeing if she remembers me," Jim said, and without another word hustled over to where Parisi was swearing under her breath at the target dummy.

"Heya. So, it turns out that you're my mom, but you probably don't remember me, because for one, you basically died when I was born, and for another, the ballerina says you don't."

Parisi stopped and narrowed her eyes on it. "Do I look like the sort of person who has demonic dog children?"

"Jim wasn't always a demon," I said quickly, feeling bad for it. "In fact, it used to be a sprite at the Court of Divine Blood. I don't suppose you remember that?"

"Of course I remember the Court. It's where many of the fellow Defenders of the Blood reside." She set her sword aside and picked up a massive two-handed battle-ax.

"Do you remember being Sovereign there?" Gabriel asked.

"Sovereign? I'm not the Sovereign; I'm a warrior." She paused, then added, "Although come to think of it, I believe someone mentioned there was a shake-up in the Court, and a new Sovereign took over."

"You were the Sovereign approximately sixteen hundred years ago," Gabriel told her.

She shook her head. "You've got me confused with someone else. I'm just a simple defender, nothing more."

A thought occurred to me at that moment. "That's exactly what we need, though. There's a very bad thane that was recently released from his prison in the Seventh Hour, and the only way we can save all the innocent mortals and immortals is to have him put back into the Hour. To do so, we need to help liberate a man named Desislav from the Akasha."

"Desislav?" She frowned, shaking her head again. "I thought ... but no. I am no Guardian. If you need someone brought from the Akasha, that's what you need."

"My demon lord is a Guardian," Jim told her.

She studied him again, then, to my happiness, knelt down and took its head in both her hands to examine its face. "I don't have a son. I would know if I did."

"You didn't get to see me much, according to Hildegarde. They took you away because they couldn't stop you from bleeding out," Jim said.

"None of this is familiar to me," she said, and stood up, apparently done with the subject.

"Jim, perhaps you would shift to human form so that your mother can see if something about you refreshes her memory," Gabriel suggested.

My eyes opened wide at his words, and while Jim answered, "OK, but I'm not going to stay like that. Dog form is just so much cooler," I whipped off my shirt, thankful I had a camisole on under it.

"Mate?" Gabriel asked as I jumped forward when Jim's form shimmered and elongated into that of an approximately six-foot-tall, stockily built, dark-haired man.

A completely naked man.

I had my shirt whipped around Jim's waist before Parisi could do more than blink, and although the shirt left its butt exposed, I tied the sleeves together behind to keep everyone from getting an eyeful.

Parisi took an involuntary step backward at the sight of Jim. She lifted a hand as if to caress its face, blinked twice, then dropped her hand.

"I'm sorry. You seem like a nice demon, but I don't know you," she told it in a softer voice than she'd used before.

"Will you help us?" Gabriel asked, and I knew he figured if we could get her out of the memory-stripping Beyond, we had a chance of restoring her past. "Saving the mortal and immortal worlds would be a fitting project for a defender of your status."

She looked dubious for a few seconds; then her brow cleared as she reached into a cloth bag sitting on a bale of hay and extracted a cell phone. "It would appear that I am free at the moment."

"Dude," Jim said to me in a whisper. "My mom has a cell phone."

"Kind of boggles the mind, huh?" I answered.

"Are you certain I can be of help?" Parisi asked. "There are so many worthy individuals who could use a defender. …"

"Absolutely," I said at the same time that Gabriel said, "We couldn't do it without you."

She thought for a moment.

"Please," Jim said, and with the emotion it bound to that one word, tears pricked behind my eyes. I gave it another quick pat to let it know Gabriel and I were there for it.

Evidently Parisi wasn't immune to the pleading in its voice, because after another few seconds' hesitation, she relented. "Very well. I can give you three days. Then I really must return, because Don Diego will take advantage of my absence to take charge of the Defenders Pilates Class should he find out I left."

"We will naturally return you to the Beyond at any time," Gabriel told her.

"Stay here," Parisi said, then disappeared into the house.

I caught Mabel eyeing Jim.

"Er …" She gave an embarrassed cough. "Would you mind me asking you why, when you are a nice-looking man—handsome, even—you take the form of a shaggy black dog?"

"I'm a Newfoundland, not a shaggy black dog," Jim said in haughty tones as it shifted back to being a shaggy black dog. "The best of all dogs, and the best being in the world. Just look at this magnificent coat. And my white chest spot. It's almost shaped like a star, which I think is telling. And I have three white toes. Got 'em the last time my form was destroyed, and I had to take a new one. I think they're kind of dashing. Here's your shirt, May."

"You keep it," I told it. The last thing I wanted was a shirt that had become intimately acquainted with Jim's junk. "I'll text Aisling and let her know what's going on."

"My apologies," Mabel told Jim, and gave it a quick pat. "You are indeed a good-looking Newfoundland. I just also think you're handsome in human form."

"Dude," Jim said with a little wiggle of its ears. "I like you and all, but I have a girlfriend. She's a Welsh corgi, and she's old and cranky and has the most adorable ears. Aisling and Amelie, Cecile's mom, are working on the magisters' union to get someone to make her immortal, because I can't even with the thought of not having my sweet little fuzzy butt with me forever. So, thanks, but I'm taken."

"Oh goddess, I wasn't … I'm not … I don't date demons … argh!" Mabel was evidently one of those people who blush easily, because she turned bright red as she stammered out an explanation. "I'm not looking for a man—or dog—so it's not a problem."

"I've always had a way with the ladies," Jim informed me in a confidential tone.

"Really?" I asked, then, thinking about its human form, had to concede. "I can see that. Mabel's right in that you are nice-looking when you're human."

"Yeah, but it's all so much trouble," it answered, then turned when Parisi emerged from the cottage.

She'd changed into what I thought of as Lord of the Rings–wear with leggings, boots, a leather doublet, and a knee-length cloak. Across her back was slung a burlap knapsack to which two swords had been strapped. She also had a bow, a couple of hunting knives tucked into her boots, a small axe attached to one hip, and, on the other, something that looked very much like a Taser.

"Is that …" I exchanged glances with Gabriel. "Is that what I think it is?"

"What is what?" Parisi looked down at herself before unclipping the Taser. "My Zapper3000? It's the very latest model. A salesman brought some to demonstrate for all the denizens of the Beyond, and I felt I needed one. I haven't had a chance to use it yet, since Don Diego was too cowardly to let me demonstrate its functions on him, but I look forward to having the opportunity to use it. Perhaps in the Akasha someone will cause us grief and I'll see if it was worth the money or not."

"They have money in the Beyond," I murmured to Gabriel.

"They have Tasers in the Beyond. I find that much more worrying," he answered at the same volume.

"Right. We need to get moving. Parisi, if you would please make the formal request for me to guide you to your next destination, we can get moving, and I can get back to my company before they fire me." Mabel held the pendant out toward Parisi. "If you would just place your hand on the moonstone while you make your request, that operates as a contract between us."

Parisi put her hand over the pendant without hesitation. "I, Parisi of Madurai, Defender of the Blood, and champion of the unheard, do hereby request that you take me to the place where I am needed."

Mabel smiled, and after she sketched a couple of symbols in the air, the pair of them lit up like several spotlights shone on them; then the light seemed to consume them before dissolving into nothing.

"That is our cue to get home," Gabriel told me, giving me a look that warned he considered our corporeal separation as ample cause for him to pleasure me to the tips of my toes once we were reunited physically. "Do you need anything?"

"Jim?" I asked, giving it the chance to speak privately.

"I mean, I'd like it if my mom remembered me, but at least I know it's this place and not me, personally," it answered. "Assuming she gets her memory back, I'm good."

"We'll head back to the portal shop," I told Gabriel, giving Jim another quick pat on the head.

"I'll meet you in London," he said before sending me another simmering look as he, too, faded to nothing.

An hour and a half later, Aisling entered her sitting room, where Gabriel and I had been indulging in some pretty steamy smooching.

"Well, we got her set—oh, lord! Sorry! I didn't know you guys were going at it," Aisling said, spinning around as she entered the room. Jim, who was behind her, snickered and pushed past her into the room.

"Wow, don't think I've ever seen Gabriel with his hand down May's shirt. Nice bra, by the way."

I tucked my breasts back into my shirt at the same time Gabriel, with a brief grimace, crossed his legs. We both glared at the demon. "We were separated," I told it. "You've lived with Aisling and Drake long enough to understand how dragons get when they're separated."

"Yeah, but you were away for just a couple of hours," Jim answered, and plopped down next to

Aisling when she decided we'd had enough chance to make ourselves decent, and took a seat on an adjacent sofa. "Like, even Ash and Drake can keep their hands off each other when Drake comes back from one of his business trips."

"That's only because we have children, and Drake is convinced that every time we are parted, the children will forget him. So when he returns, he immediately sees them to reassure himself before he tackles our time apart," Aisling said with heightened color. "What I was saying is that Parisi is established in our best spare room. I feel a little overwhelmed with the idea of having a former Sovereign as a guest, but she seems genuinely interested in helping."

"She doesn't know me, though," Jim said, and flopped onto the ground. "My own mom doesn't even remember she had me."

Aisling gave Jim a hug. "I know it hurts, but from what you guys were saying, there's a good chance that she'll get her memory back the longer we can keep her out of the Beyond. So I guess we're good to go with the next step."

"Which is what?" I asked, digging a pen out of my pocket with which to make notes. "I don't think we've really addressed getting everyone into the Thirteenth Hour. Can one visit it? Or is it truly like a prison?"

"Sorry we're late. The traffic at this time of day is insane!" Allie and Christian appeared at the door. "I don't know why I expected there to be no traffic jams in London, but it seems like that's all we encountered."

"And yet, you wish to stay here for four months," Christian told her. "Now you see why I say it is better to remain at home, where we can travel without putting up with such strife."

"I love London," Aisling and I both said at the same time.

"So do I, and next time, we'll take the tube," Allie told us as Christian and she settled onto the love seat opposite Aisling's. "What have we missed? Is Parisi here safe and sound? Did she have any helpful information? Does she think Jim's father can tackle the thane?"

"Not a lot, yes, not really, and she doesn't really seem to have an opinion on it," Aisling answered, fussing with a laptop that she placed on a sleek ebony stand against the wall, spinning it around so that it faced us all. "Right, this should be set to auto-accept people as they sign in for our meeting. We can chat until everyone is present."

"Has there been any news on the thane?" Gabriel asked Christian.

"Very little," Christian answered, his brows pulling together in a straight slash. "We have several Dark Ones hunting for him, but since we don't know what part of the world he emerged into, it's been difficult finding news of him. Our Horsemen have split up to lead teams of searchers throughout the continents."

"Horsemen?" Aisling asked.

"They are kind of an elite police force for the vampires," Allie answered. "They were originally four—and yes, they named themselves after the fabled horsemen of the apocalypse—but now there are five of them."

"Finch has been handling research from his end, and I'm sure will update us with any news he—ah. There he is."

"We are here, indeed," Finch's face popped into view on the screen, accompanied by his wife, Tatiana. "And I'm afraid if you are counting on us for information, we are sadly lacking in anything but the barest of scraps."

"Finch tried to get any details he could from the other three thanes, not that Deacon—or rather, Cadell—is being cooperative, but the other two simply refuse to talk to him."

"They claim I am one of the reasons they tried to destroy Abaddon, which is simply nonsensical, since it was their actions that resulted in them being cursed into the first Dark Ones, but they refuse to admit that," Finch said with a thinning of his lips.

"They are generally being asshats," Tatiana said with a decidedly glum air. "I think they're being stubborn on purpose. I know Deacon is. But how we are supposed to get any information from them is beyond us. You can't torture someone who's already dead."

Finch shot her a look.

"Not that we'd torture anyone," Tatiana added with a wide smile. "We're so totally not that sort of a lord and lady of the Hour. Although I wouldn't mind getting Deacon alone in a room with a couple of Tasers and a nice solid length of a rubber hose. Maybe a cattle prod, too."

Silence fell at that pronouncement, a silence that was almost pregnant in unspoken thoughts.

"Yes, well, that goes without saying," Finch said smoothly. "What news do you have of the demon dog's mother?"

"She's upstairs enjoying unthrottled Internet access," Aisling answered. "Evidently it's a bit spotty in the Beyond, so she has a hard time streaming. I believe she said she was going to binge all seasons of *Lucifer* until she was needed."

"I'm not sure how I feel about my mom having the hots for a demon lord—wait …" Jim's face scrunched up. "Never mind."

"I know exactly how I feel about her wanting to binge Tom Ellis," Aisling said. "Mmrowr."

"I second that mmrowr," Allie said, then giggled when Christian shot her an outraged look.

"Thirded," I said, leaning into Gabriel, my fingers drawing a ward on his leg. "Not that I need eye candy when Gabriel is around, but it was a good show."

"Fourthed, not that it's needed, and stop it, Finch. You just got done telling me how much you admired Mary Berry's ability with pastry, so you can't yell in my head about me liking Tom Ellis's acting."

Tatiana's lips twitched a few times as Finch protested, "I did not yell in your head. I simply pointed out that Beloveds are supposed to put their Dark One first and foremost in their thoughts."

"Which I have done, currently do, and will continue to do," she answered, pressing a kiss into his cheek. "You know full well I'm insanely in love with you."

He looked mollified, and evidently was also doing the mind-talking thing, because she stifled a couple of laughs.

"—really going to have to control it, because if I have to explain to the man at the hardware store why we need four more fire extinguishers, I will go stark, staring mad. Brom! I'm not done speaking with—by the rood, that boy is going to be the death of me. Oh, hello, everyone. Baltic! The video call has started. Would you mind putting out the chair in the corner? Brom got too close to it when he was having his hissy fit." Ysolde, who had been looking to the side, ignored a small child as he raced around the couch upon which she was seated. "Sorry for the chaos, everyone. Brom is evidently upset by something to do with you-know-who and is especially fiery of late. Also, Pavel and Holland and their baby have gone away for a long weekend break, since things have been dramatic here at Dragonwood, so Anduin is running amok. Here, lovey … you can play dragons and knights, and gut the evil Saint George. Oh! We have news! Baltic found his missing older brother."

"That is good news," Aisling said. "Was he lost, or just on his own doing Firstborn things?"

"Sounds like a bit of both," Ysolde said, glancing at Baltic as he took a seat next to her. He nodded at the men present. They all responded in kind. "I gather he was a bit overwhelmed at being out of whatever purgatory he'd placed himself. He's in the southwest US right now."

"Er …" I slid a glance toward Gabriel, but he looked as confused as I felt. "Is he doing something to find Xavier and Deus?"

"I have no idea," Ysolde said brightly. "I assume Baltic knows, because he usually knows things like that, but since he's not being at all forthcoming to the woman who he claims is the air in his lungs and blood in his veins, I couldn't say for certain."

Baltic looked like he wanted to sigh, but managed to keep hold of the urge. "I told you that I did not yet know what he intended to do, but that I was willing to discuss the situation with him when he was ready. He has not contacted me since; thus, I do not know."

The strident noise of a smoke detector started up behind them.

"You say that, but then you leave out big wads of information like what sort of person he is, and why the First Dragon went and routed him out of his purgatory, and just what he is supposed to do to help us, other than the fact that two Firstborn have to be better than one Firstborn, but I suppose that's a matter to be left until we're happy with the thane situation." While she spoke, she had been typing on her phone, no doubt to text Brom, because after almost a minute of the siren, it suddenly quieted.

"Um ..." Allie held up her hand. "I hate to sound ignorant, but I thought dragons were masters of fire. You need fire extinguishers?"

"Need? No," Baltic answered, leaning back and pulling Ysolde tighter against him. "We can control our fire as well as mundane fire, but Brom is still learning control, and forgets that dragon fire left to burn on flammable material will ultimately destroy it."

Ysolde snuggled into Baltic. "With Brom, it's all emotion-based, which is yet another thing I'd like to point out to the First Dragon. He couldn't have waited until Brom was past this stage and a bit more emotionally mature, oh no. He just had to make him a dragon when he was at his most volatile."

Baltic looked thoughtful for a moment. "Recall the years when Brom was between thirteen and fifteen, Mate."

Ysolde shuddered. "I retract my statement. Those were definitely worse years, emotionally speaking. Well, enough about us here at Dragonwood, and the ever-engaging drama of Brom and Pixie. I take it you found Jim's mother?"

A few minutes were spent catching everyone up to speed; then we settled down to make plans.

"So, I have done my homework," Aisling said when I'd finished reading out the notes. "I talked with both the head of the Guardians' Guild and my mentor, Nora, who has made a study of the history of Abaddon. Evidently, even though the Thirteenth Hour is located in the Akasha, mere Guardians can't send anyone to it.

That requires what Nora described as an almost impossible level of power and coordination to achieve."

"That's what Baltic said, although he wasn't absolutely sure that someone of your abilities might not be able to do it," Ysolde said with a cocked eyebrow.

"I mentioned that to Caribbean Battiste, the head of our order, and he said that although he thought that a savant like me might actually be able to pull it off, it would come at a seriously high cost. Think proscription level of cost." Aisling made a face. "Been there, done that, don't want to have to go through it again. Not to mention the fact that Drake would never allow me to do anything so risky. So, we're going to have to rely on Mabel to transport Team Parisi into the place, since reapers can access any underworld, and the Thirteenth Hour is definitely one."

"Which means getting out is going to be even harder," I said thoughtfully before turning to Gabriel. "Would we be able to help?"

He thought about it for half a minute before shaking his head in obvious reluctance. "I wish I could say that the dragonkin were a match for whatever security measures are in place in that Hour, but would be foolish to doom us."

"This is not a dragon fight—" Christian started to say.

"But Rowan and Sophea fought all those challenges in the Egyptian underworld—my apologies, Christian." Aisling made an apologetic gesture. "I didn't mean to run over your objection, but I wanted to point out that at least in the Duat, dragons reign supreme."

"The Thirteenth Hour is not the Duat," Baltic said in his usual cryptic manner. "But that is not the biggest issue with this plan."

Christian gave him a quick nod of approval. "The dragon speaks correctly. Getting into the Hour is not the problem."

"You mean that getting out is the problem. We'll have Parisi and Desi to get them and Jim and whoever else helps out of the Akasha," Aisling pointed out. "In other words, very respectable powerhouses. I think the two of them joined together should be able to do the job."

"Whereas I feel the real difficulty lies in the fact that you are not certain they will work together," Christian argued. "And if they do not, then whoever you send with the demon's mother may well be trapped there."

Silence, thick and uncomfortable, fell over the room.

"Well, hell," Aisling said.

"Abaddon," murmured Jim, now leaning into my leg, moaning softly as I scratched under its collar.

"I hadn't thought of that, but you are absolutely correct," Gabriel said, his brow furrowed. "And no, May, you will not be part of any group that attempts to rescue Jim's father."

I pinched his thigh. "You know better than to tell me what I can and can't do."

He cocked an eyebrow at me, and allowed one of his dimples to deepen.

"Dammit, you also know I'm helpless against your dimples," I told him, and gave him as chaste a kiss as I could manage in front of the others. "I admit I wasn't looking forward to going to any part of the Akasha, but I am happy to help in any way I can."

"What about Hunter?" Ysolde asked, having been momentarily called upon to admire her son's toy horse. "He said he'd help."

"He is needed," Baltic said, and, when we all looked at him, donned his inscrutable expression.

"Needed—oh, Xavier. I can't believe I forgot about him for a moment." Aisling rubbed her forehead.

"What we need is yet another demigod," Ysolde said, *oof*ing a little when Anduin clambered across her to Baltic, where he galloped his horse up and down Baltic's leg. "One who can make sure that everyone who goes in comes out … with Desislav the Destroyer."

"There are no more demigods," Allie said, then gave a little head tip. "That is to say, I'm sure there are oodles more of them, but none that we know. Although …" She stopped and glanced at Christian. "What about that woman who helped Alec and Cora? She was pretty powerful, Alec said. I mean, she and Cora banished Bael to the Akasha. That takes pretty big chops to do that."

Christian's expression shifted into one almost identical to Baltic's. "Sally was the Sovereign. That is why she was able, with the help of the Tools of Bael, to banish him."

"Sally," Gabriel said with a lot of speculation, his gaze resting on me. "She certainly once had the power to do what we'd need, but does she still?"

"On it!" Aisling said, picking up her phone, then hesitated. "Does anyone have her number?"

"I did, but the last time we called her—when we were all looking for Asmodeus's ring—it apparently was mysteriously disconnected."

Jim got up and, without a word, walked over to where it had a plush dog bed, alongside a low table containing some of its magazines, a tablet, and console game controllers, and returned with a phone. "I got it. Here."

Aisling stared at her demon. "How on earth do you have Sally's phone number?"

It cocked a furry eyebrow at her. "How do you think I have it? She gave it to me."

"Why?" I couldn't help but ask, aware that, despite my better intentions, I was mildly annoyed that Sally would rather let Jim have her number than us.

"We go way back, Sally and me," was all it said before making faces at Aisling's laptop, which in turn made Anduin (now back on Ysolde's lap) laugh hysterically. "She helped me with a problem a while back and got the job done so well that we still laugh about it today."

"What problem did you have?" Aisling asked, clearly concerned. "Was it after I summoned you?"

"Naw, this was before we met." It gave her a long, considering look. "But Sally did good. She could totes handle stuffing us into the Hour."

"We will circle back to your problems that only Sally can solve when we're alone. Right, I'm sending her a text asking her to talk to us. … What's the link … ? Got it. OK, fingers crossed she gets this and can chat or, worst-case scenario, will talk to us later. What's next on our Catch the Thane Increasingly Complex Plan?" Aisling asked, looking at me.

"I got nothing," I said, holding up my notebook to show her a blank page. "Although I do have to say that I have some issues with us asking Sally to help. For one, she isn't at all straightforward. She's as twisty as they come. And for another—"

"She'll want to touch Gabriel, yes, we know," Ysolde said. "But you won't let that happen, so it's a moot point. Are there any other objections to asking Sally for help? Baltic?"

"What?" he asked, once again in possession of their son, along with a massive picture book.

"Do you think Sally has the ability to help us?" she asked.

Baltic lifted one shoulder a fraction of an inch. "As a Sovereign? Yes. That doesn't mean she will, however."

"Handsome as the day is long, and so smart." A light, annoyingly chirpy, and extremely Southern gracious-lady voice filled the room at the same time a new square popped up on the call screen. "I tell you, if I wasn't romantically entangled with a deliciously wicked unicorn, I'd search through the dragonkin for one of you sexy dragons. May, darlin'! And you have the delectable Gabriel sitting right there where anyone can ogle his manly thighs. What a charming meeting. Please do invite me to more."

"Hello, Sally," I said, trying to keep my voice even and not in any way reflecting the irritation that seemed to dog her appearance in my life.

"Welcome," Ysolde said, momentarily distracted when Baltic took a couple of obvious sniffs as their son wrestled with the book, then turned to her. "Nope. I'm busy with the meeting. You can help him use the potty."

"You asked me to be here, as well," Baltic pointed out, grimacing when Anduin climbed over him, evidently hitting tender parts in the process. "You said my insight was invaluable."

"So is potty training. We're at the cusp. He's almost there. He just needs a little more attention, and then it'll click," she answered.

With only the barest hint of an eye roll, Baltic snagged his son and, tucking him under one arm, marched off-screen with him.

"I have to say, having seen firsthand just how … intense … Baltic was before he found you, the sight of him doing diaper duty is … well, it's kind of weird," I admitted. "I mean, he was the dread wyvern. Now he's a dad."

"Eh," Ysolde said, waving it away. "He's still the baddest of all the dragon badasses. He simply values family over everything else. But we got off the point. Sally, it's always nice to see you, but this time, we have a very particular situation, and we think you could be of vital assistance."

"Really?" She tipped her head to the side, her eyes bright with speculation. "Does it have something to do with the silent vampires and their Beloveds?"

"If we're silent, it's only because we're awaiting orders," Finch answered.

"Sorry," Allie said, returning from the hall where she and Christian had slipped out to take a call. "The girls insisted on singing Christian the latest song they wrote, and you truly don't want to hear that. For that matter, *I* don't want you to hear it lest you ban me from the mates, etc. group."

"Allegra," Christian protested. "They wrote a song for me. What other children of that age can do such a thing?"

"It's not their composition I object to. It's the fact that they inherited my tin ear and even tinnier vocal cords, and yet insist on singing at the top of their voices." Allie paused for a second before retaking her seat. "I apologize again. You didn't need to hear any of this argument."

"I find it fascinating," Aisling said, tucking her legs under her. "It's so nice to see how other beings raise their kids. I'm delighted to know that you go through the same crap we do."

"Literally, in Baltic's case," Ysolde said with a blithe unconcern that always made me want to laugh. "Perhaps May could recap quickly for Sally?"

I could, and did, and three and a half minutes later, I finished somewhat exhausted.

"Much though I appreciate you thinkin' of me for this caper, I feel obligated to tell you that I couldn't possibly break into the Thirteenth Hour. It's run by the Court, you know," Sally said, giving a little shake of her head.

"We know, but we hoped that since you're no longer Sovereign, you could see your way clear to helping get our party to Jim's father," Gabriel said.

"I couldn't. I really couldn't," she said, giving another headshake. "The amount of trouble I'd get into if I tried—it fair boggles the brainmeats."

"But—" Aisling started to say.

"Sugar, May will tell you that I am nothing if not devoted to you-all, but just because I was once one-half of the Sovereign doesn't mean I can tamper with the Akasha. I do still have to uphold Court policy." Sally stretched and did a few head bobs to the side. "Now, if that's all you wanted, I have a goat yoga class, and today is my turn with the goat with horns, so I can't be late."

"You have always rejoiced in being obstreperous," I couldn't help but say, annoyed that she wouldn't even hear us out before rejecting our request.

"Mayling," Gabriel said in a tone meant to remind me that although Sally might no longer be Sovereign, she did still command respect.

"Well, I'm sorry, but she is," I said, wanting to say a lot more, but managed to keep it behind my teeth.

"It's not obstreperousness, darlin' May—it's just me being a little naughty," Sally said, her smile filled with more teeth than looked normal. "I have always enjoyed being naughty. It's satisfying on so many levels."

"There's nothing more naughty than going against millennia of old doctrine," Jim said from where it was lying on the floor.

"Effrijim!" Sally said, blowing it a kiss and giving it another of her impossible smiles. "I didn't see you there. As for the doctrine of the Court … it's beyond me to change it."

"If I were in your shoes," Jim said, idly scratching an ear, "and I wanted to indulge in my wild side, then I'd be the first in line to help break Desi out. I mean, something like that is going to make you famous throughout the Otherworld."

Sally froze for a fraction of a second. It went so fast that I almost didn't catch it. "Desi?" she asked, her eyes narrowing as she leaned forward. "As in Desislav the Destroyer?"

"Yes, that's who we need your help to release," Aisling said.

"We're hoping that he'll help us with our thane issue," Allie added. "He's really pivotal to our plan, so we kind of need him."

A male voice rumbled in Ysolde's square. She turned to the side, obviously listening to Baltic before she faced us again, and asked, "Baltic would like to know if you are acquainted with Desislav, Sally? Personally, that is?"

"Yes," she said slowly. I had the feeling she was sorting through memories to find what she wanted. "I knew him back before he even thought of the idea of Abaddon. He was so handsome, and had an intriguing darkness within him that was almost impossible to resist. All us cherubim had crushes on him, so that whenever we crossed paths, he'd have a gaggle of us following him around like cats chasing a milkmaid."

"Great," Jim said, its head now on the floor. "Sally has the hots for my dad. Like this couldn't get any more implausible?"

"Plausibility is overrated," Ysolde said dismissively. "Does this mean you'll help us, Sally?"

To my surprise, Sally didn't hesitate. "Yes, I believe that now you've made the situation clear, I will be able to take you to the Hour. But it will cost you."

"We will pay whatever sum you request," Christian said in his plummy accent.

"So handsome. Really, I must look outside the Court for dating material," Sally murmured to herself before saying, "The cost is not one that can be fulfilled by money. Instead, I would ask for a boon as compensation for taking you to the Thirteenth Hour."

"What sort of boon?" I asked suspiciously, narrowing my eyes at her. She returned the gesture.

"I don't know yet, but when I do, you'll be the very first one to hear," she said with what I thought of as her smug-ass tone.

"That is not acceptable," Christian said, bending upon her a stern look that I wouldn't want to have directed at me. "We will not agree to such a vague definition."

"Take it or leave it," she answered in the same annoying tone. I fought to keep from grinding my teeth at her. "I will help you for an as-yet-unnamed boon."

"Done," Ysolde said quickly. "We agree to your terms."

"No, we don't. Rather, the Moravian Council does not agree to such nebulous terms." Christian was clearly fired up now, his eyes almost glowing with ire.

"His eyes are almost as bright as yours," I whispered to Gabriel. "But yours are much, much warmer."

"That's because I have a mate who keeps my fire burning hot," he answered, sliding one hand down my back until it curled under my left butt cheek.

"I believe that since this is a joint project between the dragons and Dark Ones, it would be fair to divide the responsibility for fulfilling the terms of the boon between us." Aisling nodded toward the screen. "Since Drake isn't here to speak for the green dragons, I'll leave it to Gabriel and Baltic to decide if that sounds reasonable and fair for everyone."

Sally had been looking at her phone during the last few comments, and said quickly, "I've got to take a quick call. I'll be right back." Her square went black as she dropped off the call.

"The Dark Ones will, naturally, assume full responsibility for payment of any kind," Christian said sternly. "There is no question of sharing the burden."

I looked at Gabriel, since Baltic—now back next to Ysolde—was being his usual silent self. Gabriel said, "I believe Christian has the right to assume the debt if the release of Jim's parents was solely to benefit the Dark Ones, but as it is possible that they might also be of assistance to the dragonkin, then it makes sense to share the cost of freeing them."

"How would Jim's parents help us?" Aisling asked, texting what I suspected was a message to Drake.

Gabriel said nothing.

"Don't even start thinking you can be as inscrutably annoying as Baltic," I told Gabriel.

"Hey, now!" Ysolde said, glaring at me.

Gabriel laughed, and pinched my butt. "I have no intention of annoying anyone, let alone my mate, but I don't know that I can answer Aisling's question. It's merely a thought I had regarding the likelihood of Jim's parents having the desire to assist us with Xavier and Deus."

To the obvious surprise of everyone, Baltic nodded at what Gabriel was saying. "That thought was on my mind, as well. Not that I wish to involve the light dragons, but Ysolde will not let us live a life of peace and happiness, and must have us involved in all weyr business."

"That's right, and we both know it's good for you, if only to stop your father from popping in and throwing cryptic demands at me before poofing into a fine sparkle of gold. I can't tell you how frustrating those damned cryptic demands are." Ysolde was evidently riled up, because Baltic pulled her up against him again before whispering something in her ear.

Christian's frown was prodigious. "Again, I must protest that this is an issue for the Moravian Council and Dark Ones to deal with—"

"I think now is the time to let go of a little of your pride and accept that our new friends are going to help us whether or not you want them to," Allie said with laughter lacing her voice, but it quickly took a more somber tone. "I, for one, am happy to get help dealing with someone who could do irreparable damage to the mortal world. I couldn't stomach the thought of innocent people suffering because we were too proud to accept the offer of help."

Christian turned an irritated expression on her. For a moment, he said nothing, although Allie smiled again, so I assumed he was mentally speaking with her. "I dislike it when you use logic against me," he finally said, then grimaced when he heard the words. "And now I sound like the worst sort of supercilious fool. Very well, since Allegra has pointed out that I can't think only of the Dark Ones, I will gracefully accept the aid that you dragons wish to offer."

"I'm so glad that's finally settled," Aisling said with a bright smile. "Now we can go ahead and book—"

"My apologies. I had to see if someone was available. But all is well there, so I just need the go-ahead to put things into motion." Sally popped back onto the screen, winking at us all, although the last sentence and gesture were clearly directed at me.

"Oh, OK," I said. Christian and Allie were momentarily absorbed looking at a text on his phone, but no one else spoke up. I slid a glance to my side. Gabriel told me earlier that since I felt strongly about helping the vampires, he would remain in a support role unless I asked him otherwise, which mean I might as well answer Sally. "We have indeed agreed to your terms, although it goes without saying that we'd appreciate a heads-up when you know what it is you want from us."

"Excellent!" she said with a clap of her hands. "I look forward to seeing Desi again. I will need exactly twenty-eight minutes; then I will meet you at the public toilets in Hyde Park. The one near the Princess Diana memorial."

"My apologies," Allie said as Christian tucked away his phone. "The kids are being absolute monsters… well, we won't go into that. I think they'll leave us alone for a few minutes."

"If you don't mind—" was all Christian got out before Sally logged off. He swore in what I thought was German. "I am not comfortable with this plan to put members of the dragon septs at risk. The point of this being our problem aside, I, like you all, do not wish to place others into situations of peril."

"If you are concerned about Sally not being able to get Jim and the reaper out, you can rest your mind," Gabriel answered after a nod from me. "Both May and I are familiar with Sally's abilities and have full confidence in them."

"OK, Mabel says she'll meet us at the bathroom in Hyde Park." Aisling tapped an answering text. "I told her we had a former Sovereign to help get everyone out if Jim's parents don't have the oomph or desire to do so. She's impressed with our connections."

"Why the bathroom?" Allie asked, hurriedly turning off her phone when a video popped up showing a dark-haired boy of about ten who had the same mismatched eyes that she had. He was doing an odd wiggly sort of dance that I suspected had its origins in popular gaming.

"Entrance," Aisling, Ysolde, and I answered at the same time.

"To this Thirteenth Hour?" Allie asked, looking incredulous. "Why would an entrance be put in a public place where there are mortals all over?"

"The actual entrance is bound to be warded so that mortals can't see it. Or rather, they can, but their brains refuse to process it, so they ignore its presence." Aisling glanced down at a ping. "And Drake's on his way back to London. I hope we can get this done before his plane gets here."

"Why?" I couldn't help but ask.

She made a face. "He gets so difficult when it comes to me dealing with any being who poses the slightest risk. Not that I'm going into the Hour, but if you need emergency Guardian services, I'm happy to leap into the fray."

"We'll see everyone off," I said after a brief confab with Gabriel. "Not that we can help with the Hour, but just in case there's something we can do outside of it, we'll be ready."

"I'll be there, of course, because I have to bring Jim and Parisi," Aisling said with a nod toward us.

"So will we. Since, as Christian has pointed out numerous times, it is our problem that you're all kindly helping with. We'll see you all in twenty-four minutes," Allie said, glancing at her watch. "There's just enough time to threaten the kids with the direst of repercussions if they even think of interrupting us again."

Everyone logged off and headed out. Gabriel went off to inform Maata and Tipene that we were going to Hyde Park. I sat for a moment thinking about putting all our eggs into the Sally basket.

It made me nervous.

It made me very nervous.

ELEVEN
Parisi

Midsummer

"My Sovereign, there is a—what is the matter?" Mags stopped and stared at where I was on my knees before the privy, emptying out my stomach with only the slightest of moans. "Are you unwell? Was it clam soup? You didn't eat any of the mushrooms that Old Grig picked, did you? I swear that man is trying to poison the Court. I tell the apprentices time and time again to never eat anything Old Grig gives them, but do they listen? No, they do not. They must needs eat the mushroom soup, and mushroom pottage, and mushrooms with eggs, and mushrooms sat gently upon a bit of salmon, over which melted butter and herbs are poured, and then they spend the next day on their knees just as you are right now. Well. You'll feel better for a bit of a purge, I reckon."

I looked up, wiping my mouth on a cloth. "I need you to take a message for me, Mags."

"I'll get you some goat's milk. ... A message?" She spun around to give me a look of dismay. "No. No, no, no. Not again. I will not go there again."

"I wouldn't ask you if it wasn't important that I speak to Desi."

"Pfft," she said, waving away my statement. "You just want to end your relationship with him. Again. For the fiftieth time."

"It hasn't been fifty times," I said wearily, pulling myself up onto the bed. "Forty at the most."

"It's been five hundred and some years that you insist you're done with him, and then a quarter year later, there you are traipsing off to see him with a song on your lips and flowers in your hair." Mags's lips closed so tight they were almost invisible. "You're just tormenting yourself with that one. He will never change."

"He has already changed," I said, eyeing the privy, unsure if my stomach was done ridding itself of the bread and porridge I'd eaten in the morn. "And that's made things harder for us both. He's struggling with the princes of Abaddon since they've added even more of them. The only way Desi retains control against their combined strength is via his relic."

"He's still evil, and stands against everything we work for," Mags insisted as she *tsk*ed when I lurched to the privy again.

"He's not," I mumbled after retching up nothing. "He's been working hard to shift the focus of Abaddon from all the heinous acts the princes perform to something less harmful. The princes are furious, because they can't stop him, but they keep trying. Oh lord. This is horrible. How am I going to survive this for the next six months?"

"Six ..." Mags gasped in a huge quantity of air. "You're with child? His child?"

I sank onto the floor, leaning against the bed, too tired and ill to do more than say, "Yes, we will be having a child. It is a blessing, I know, but right now …" The words trailed off. I couldn't rally the energy needed to finish the thought.

"You don't know what you have done," Mags said, shaking her head even as she helped me back onto my bed before tucking me in. "I fear you are going to regret many things in the future, my Sovereign."

"I already have," I murmured, and willed myself to sleep.

* * *

Desi
Winter Solstice

Editor's note: the text contained in the hidebound journal kept by Parisi of Madurai is partially damaged, and some words are illegible due to water splotches. The editor has done her best in making coherent sentences in those cases.

My beloved Parisi is dying. She asked me to make note of the events of this day in her journal, and I will do so only because I have sworn to do whatever she asks of me.

In the middle of the night, Parisi's woman fetched Desi from Abaddon, telling him, "My beloved Sovereign has asked for you. I told her that to have one as you around her would only suck the good miasma away from her body, but she insists."

"She has started birthing?" he asked as he flung her up on a fresh horse, and mounted his own.

"Yes. Several hours ago." Mags's voice wobbled as they set off at a speed Desi knew they couldn't keep for long. Fortunately, Parisi had caused a little-known portal to the Court to be made within an hour's ride of the Bali entrance to Abaddon. "All is not going well. She sent me to fetch you in case …"

Desi refused to finish her sentence, either mentally or out loud. It seemed to take both forever and no time before he followed Mags into the entrance, and was immediately hustled into a darkened room pierced by pools of flickering light.

"My love," he said, clutching at Parisi's hand where she lay propped up on a number of pillows. Her face was pale and damp, tendrils of her hair clinging to her sweaty face. "My life, my heart, my sun and moon."

"Always so dramatic," she answered, her voice rough as if she'd been screaming. She turned to look at him, a small smile curling the edges of her mouth. "But I am glad you are here to see our child born."

"Is there no water to wipe her face?" he asked when she sank back into her pillows, obviously exhausted. The thin shift she wore was glued to her body, the mound of her belly making him feel simultaneously happy and terrified. What if something happened to her or the babe? "Where is the midwife? Can nothing be done for Parisi's distress? Are there no medicines?"

Mags had been in the corner, speaking with an aged woman who looked to be as old as the rocks that made up the walls of Parisi's keep. All others had been sent from the room, no doubt to keep them from becoming aware of his presence. The old woman shuffled forward, gesturing toward him. He frowned, unsure of what she wanted before Parisi said, "That is Aurora, our wise-woman. She wishes you to kneel before her."

Instantly, Desi felt irritated that some old woman thought he would so debase himself before her—he was Desislav the Destroyer, prince of Abaddon, and lord of seven hundred legions. He did not kneel before anyone.

The old lady stopped before him. He knelt, forcing himself to be passive when she took his chin in her hand and studied him with eyes that were clouded white. For a moment, he felt something akin to panic as she saw through to his soul ... and the tally of sins he had committed in his long life.

"You have much darkness in you, but it is countered by the light that shines from your soul," the old woman said, releasing his chin to shuffle over to Parisi.

"Him?" Mags asked, sounding as surprised as he was. "Light? He has light in his soul? Are you sure it is not merely a reflection from our beloved Sovereign?"

Parisi moaned then, and clutched the bedclothes beneath her.

"Get behind her and help her push," the old lady told him. He complied, whispering into Parisi's ears just how much he loved her, and how she was his everything. That started what he mentally called the period of screaming, when Parisi was trying to push from her body their child.

It was afternoon before the babe was born. He barely glanced when the midwife Aurora showed him a blotchy face almost obliterated by the soft linen wrap that wound around him.

"My love? We have a son," he told Parisi. She lay back on the pillows, her body drenched and heaving as she panted, tears mingling with sweat on her face.

She smiled despite her obvious exhaustion, a smile unlike any he had ever seen, filling him with piercing joy as she said, "A son. We have a son. Show him to me."

Aurora, who had been attending to the cord, laid the babe gently in her arms. Parisi made noises that

Desi had never heard, odd little coos that seemed to bind him to her and the babe in a way he could never imagine.

He spent the next day there, hidden in her chamber so the Court would not know their most hated foe was present.

She has not stopped bleeding since the birth. It has been a day, and still, she bleeds, and with each passing hour, she grows more pale and weaker. I despair. I begged the midwife to do whatever she needed to stop the bleeding.

After a day, Mags took me aside and said Parisi was dying.

Desi railed and begged and promised the healers and midwife untold riches if they would stop the bleeding, but they could do little.

"She has to go into the Beyond," Mags told Desi in a whisper on the second night after the birth. "She is failing, Lord Desi. You can see that as well as I can."

"She'll get better," he said, ignoring the desperation in his voice. "She can't die, not of this. She's the Sovereign."

"Even immortal beings can die if they have no blood left in their bodies," Mags said, her own eyes swimming.

He felt her grief, but could do no more than acknowledge it with a squeeze to her shoulder before turning to look at Parisi.

Mags was right. She was dying. She had to go into the Beyond. But that would leave him with the babe—

"Effrijim? Where is Effrijim?" Parisi struggled to sit up, her eyes glazed as she looked wildly around the room.

"He is with a wet nurse," Desi told her, taking a damp cloth to wipe her face before gently easing an arm behind her. "My love … the bleeding …" His throat closed around the words.

"I know," she answered, her voice scarcely more than a whisper. "Mags said I should diminish into the Beyond, and I will do so, but not before seeing our son again."

He gestured toward the woman, who nodded and hurried out of the chamber. He continued to hold Parisi, mindless of the tears that rolled down his cheeks as he buried his face in her hair, his soul screaming out in anguish.

"You will visit me?" she asked, turning slightly in his arms so she could face him. "Where I settle in the Beyond? You will bring Effrijim so that I may see him grow?"

"Yes," he lied, not wanting her to hear how the L'au-dela, the newly formed organization that ran the Beyond—amongst other things—recently wove protections into the Beyond against those who bore dark power, like him. He knew that once she diminished, he'd never see her again. "Yes, we will see you often. As often as you like."

"Good," she said, sagging back, her eyes closing. "So long as we aren't separated."

Tears splashed onto his hand as it held hers, his throat being choked with sorrow.

Mags brought in the babe, and Parisi held him for a long time, talking to the babe and telling him how much she loved him, and that he would be fine with Desi.

It almost killed him, but Desi pushed the sorrow and grief and pain down deep so he could give Parisi a serene countenance when she reached for him.

Four litter bearers had arrived to carry her to the entrance of the Beyond. He knew with every morsel of his being that the only way he could provide happiness for her was a sacrifice, and he committed to it without a second's hesitation.

As the men lifted the litter, he leaned over Parisi to adjust a blanket, knowing full well that when she diminished into the Beyond, she would be bound by grief and sorrow. He placed one hand on her cheek as he brushed his lips against hers. In his other hand, he held the blood moon, and drawing on its power, he whispered into her mouth, "You are the love of my life, and I cannot let you suffer heartbreak, not for a moment, and not for the rest of your life. Fare you well, my beloved. Forget this world, and thrive and find joy in your new life."

Her eyes opened at his words, but as the spell took hold of her, her gaze softened, and became confused.

She was borne off to join a formal procession with all the denizens of the Court leading her to her new domain. Desi stood in the now-empty room, feeling as if he were made of glass and the slightest breeze would shatter him into a million pieces.

"She will not suffer," Mags told him from the doorway.

"No, she will not," he answered, his voice choked. "Nor will our son. I will see to that."

Mags shot him a glance and seemed to understand. "You wish for him to be raised here in the Court?"

"Yes." He tried not to think of the sleeping child in the next room. He loved that small, blotchy bundle almost as much as he loved Parisi, but knew what had to be done. "If you will do so, I would be grateful."

"My Sovereign would want it that way, if the babe could not be with you." Mags continued to watch him, evidently seeing through to the darkness that he began pulling on to keep the pain at bay long enough for him to do what he must.

He said nothing more, leaving the Court to return back to his own home.

Night was falling when he faced the other princes.

"You have long sought to get hold of the blood moon," he said, striding into the hall to the head of a long table, around which sat Hath, Wat, Bael, Amaymon, and Ariton, the last two of whom were the newest additions to Abaddon. He pulled off the chain upon which the stone was hung, and slammed it onto the table, making sure he met the gaze of each man there before continuing. "I am willing to trade it and control of Abaddon."

"Trade? For what?" Hath asked, scowling.

"I will leave. Relinquish my legions. Accept banishment from Abaddon. And in exchange, you will commit an oath upon the blood moon that no harm will befall my child, named Effrijim."

Pandemonium followed as all the princes spoke at once, demanding explanations, arguing amongst themselves, and peppering Desi with a dozen questions.

He held up his hand and was about to repeat his offer when Bael rose from the table and strolled over to the massive fireplace against the north wall. "Your terms are acceptable to us, with one exception."

"No harm must befall my child, no matter what the circumstances, for the duration of his life and afterlife. Without that oath, the blood moon remains with me," Desi said in a tone that bristled with warning.

"A child," Bael said, waving away the idea of Desi's sweet—if blotchy—child. "A child is of no matter to us. But you ... you *are* a matter."

"I said that I would accept banishment from Abaddon," he pointed out, pushing hard on the emotions that once again threatened to overwhelm him. He'd spent several hours with his son earlier, trying to commit to his memory everything about him before it was time to make the sacrifice. Mags had been unusually kind to him, helping him feed the babe with goat's milk before he had to leave. He took what solace he could when Mags swore to him that Effrijim would be cherished and loved by the entire Court. "That must suffice. Without the blood moon, I have no power here."

"Not here, but elsewhere. No, I believe that Abaddon cannot continue to thrive if its founder—relicless as you would be—can simply return to take over anytime he desires."

"I couldn't even if I wanted," Desi replied, anger driving out some of the pain.

"Thus," Bael continued, examining a few silver pieces upon the mantel, "speaking as I do for the other princes, I will accept your terms with the exception that, instead of being banished from Abaddon, you be banished to the Akasha. The Thirteenth Hour, to be exact. It is ruled over by the Court of Divine Blood, a fitting captor, do you not think?"

Desi ignored the sly dig, well aware that at least two of the princes knew about his dalliance with Parisi. Idly, he wondered when Bael had taken up the mantle of leader. He'd been so caught up with Parisi and the babe ever since she told him he was to become a father that he hadn't been paying attention to the politics of the other princes. "It matters little where I go."

In the end, though, he mused as he strolled over to where Bael was examining a gold goblet, he would suffer untold misery for the rest of his life being separated from the two people who held his heart, so he didn't care if he was miserable out in the mortal world or locked away in the Akasha.

He plucked the goblet from Bael's hands and replaced it on the mantel.

"So be it," he said, and gestured to his steward, who promptly pulled out two large pieces of vellum upon which had been written the contract. Alongside them, a small but sharp dagger was set before the steward bowed his way out of the room.

"The blood moon?" Bael said, holding out his hand.

"Sign first; then I will relinquish it." Desi met Bael's gaze, and recognized the power that crackled around him. Somehow, the former dragon had managed to gain a significant amount of dark power. The thought flitted through Desi's head that if Bael kept the relic for himself, he might well become impossible to overthrow. "Not my problem now," he murmured as he watched the five princes sign both contracts in their own blood, binding them to its terms with an unbreakable blood oath.

Desi picked up the chain holding the blood moon and, after tracing his thumb over it one last time, set it on one of the contracts, nicked his finger, and signed.

Then, with a look at all five princes, he collected one of the vellum copies and left Abaddon, immediately falling into a deep, dark abyss.

TWELVE
Sally

"I figured they'd call you in on this."

Sally smiled at the phone as she hurried across the velvety green expanse of grass in the corner of Hyde Park, heading for the men's toilet block. "You have learned exceptionally quick, Sasha. How are things going there?"

"Fine and dandy. The stable cat had another litter of kittens, and that makes two in two years, so I'm going to take her in to have her fixed. One of the kittens has orange stripes." Sasha, the current Sovereign of the Court, had what Sally thought of as maxed-out eccentricity trait. She was quirky beyond quirky, although Sally had to admit that it was one of her charms.

"I've always enjoyed people who march to the beat of their own drummer," she said aloud.

"Me, too. Drummers are always so sexy. And they have good rhythm. So, you just called to tell me you're going to breach one of the most revered tenets of the Court?"

"Well, of course, darlin'!" Sally saw in the distance two familiar figures heading toward the area that contained the toilets. "You didn't think I was going to spring Desislav the Destroyer without telling you."

"It goes against everything the Court stands for," Sasha said, somewhat muffled as if she was rubbing an orange-striped kitten on her face. "It violates at least three Court dictates that I can think of."

"I can think of six, but that doesn't really matter, does it?" Sally hurried toward the low building just visible through a clump of trees and shrubs.

"I suppose not," Sasha answered, sounding somewhat thoughtful. "Not that I could stop you if I wanted, but I do feel obligated as current Sovereign to remind you that by freeing a man deemed so evil by his own fellow princes of Abaddon they banished him to the Akasha, you may well be releasing an apocalypse upon the mortal world."

"They've faced worse," Sally replied, then was forced by curiosity to ask, "You don't think you could stop me?"

"Nope."

She thought about that for a moment, then smiled at nothing. "I must remember to tell Terrin. He will be so pleased."

"Really?" Sasha asked.

"Of course. He is the most powerful of the two of us. I was always just the showy one. He much preferred to stay in the background and manipulate things to give people the best chance at succeeding."

"That's why I asked him to continue what he was doing—unofficially, to avoid red tape," Sasha said, murmuring softly to what Sally imagined was the mama cat as she gave back the kitten. "He's been busy taking care of a revolt amongst the mages. The magister people thought we could help, so Terrin decided to tackle the problem."

"I never found mages revolting," Sally mused. "It's their shoes, I think. They always look so expensive."

The silence that resulted from that statement told her Sasha clearly didn't follow her logic, but she didn't have the time to explain her personal philosophy regarding shoes and the nature of the human spirit. "I see May and her handsome dragon, and I believe the demon Effrijim is just ahead of her, so I must leap into action. Do you have anything you wish for me to pass along to them?"

Sasha gave a hint of a chuckle. "Other than my hope they aren't releasing death upon the mortal and immortal worlds? No. I'm sure you'll do what is necessary."

"Me?" Sally was pleased with the level of disbelief she managed to squeeze into one word. "I'm only there to get them to Desislav."

"I have always admired your ability to stick your fingers into things and not be seen doing so."

"Darlin'!" Sally said, pleased with the flattery. "Someone has been studying Court records for the last few hundred years."

"It's like having a master class in constructive deception," Sasha agreed. "I'd wish you good luck with your endeavor, but we both know how little luck has to do with anything you set your mind to. So instead, I'll simply say, later, tater."

Sally paused for a moment to send a text to Terrin.
ME
Sasha says you are doing covert work amongst the mages. We both know you harbor nothing but distrust for them. I distinctly remember you ranting in the early eighteenth century about how they need to be monitored lest they run amok. I am shocked at you agreeing to sort them out now.

TERRIN

She also says you are going to spring Desislav the Destroyer from the Lake of Upside-Down Sinners. Of the two of us, which one is doing something shocking?

ME

Love you, too. Smooches!

She tucked her phone away before lifting her hand in response when the demon Jim popped out of the bathroom to stare at her in what she imagined was a chastising manner.

"Heya," the demon said to her. "Wow. You really got into that *Barbie* movie, didn't you? I don't think I've seen anyone dressed head to toe in that shade of pink."

She paused to do a little spin. "Thank you. It's my new favorite power suit."

"I don't think people call them—never mind," Jim said, then followed when Sally picked her way around to a small clearing behind the men's toilet. The group of people who stood there turned confused expressions on her. "Hello, everyone. Are we all here? Those of us going into almost certain death, destruction, and possible perpetual torment?"

May looked horrified, while Gabriel's lips twitched. She smiled to herself at that. He was far more astute than was first obvious. The Guardian Aisling also didn't look fooled by her lighthearted banter.

"Yup, we're all here. This is Mabel. I don't think you've met her." Aisling introduced a young redhead.

"A reaper? How pleasant. I had lunch a few months ago with the head of your order," Sally told the woman, who stood looking very uncomfortable. She wondered why, but decided that mystery would have to wait.

"And this is Parisi," Aisling said, gesturing toward the tall, dark-haired woman who was clad in metal breastplate beautifully etched with fantastical figures. She also wore a chain skirt that hung down to her knees, black leggings, and a bum bag bearing a psychedelic peace sign. A massive sword was strapped to her back, along with a bow, and what looked very much like a small beheading axe. "Er … I'm not sure if you know her or not."

Parisi, who had been staring intently into the shrubberies, turned to face Sally.

She felt the impact of that look, and the irrelevant part of her mind—which admittedly claimed most of the available space—noted that Parisi held a form of power that was both unfamiliar and almost overwhelming. Immediately, she made a low formal bow, the sort that she hadn't made since she had first met Terrin. "My Sovereign, it is a pleasure to meet you."

Parisi studied her for a moment, then smiled. "You are with the Court. Welcome, fellow defender. You should be of great help when dealing with the prisoner."

"That's why I get paid the big money," Sally answered, then beamed at the rest of the company.

"Are we going soon? I don't want to sound like a parrot with only one phrase, but I really do have responsibilities I must attend to this afternoon." While Mabel the reaper spoke, Sally had a momentary sense of dark power. She gave her a good stare before catching Jim doing the same.

It really was a very astute demon at times. Not often, she told herself as she gave it a swift pat on the head, but there were times when it clearly saw things that the others didn't.

"Is there anything we can do out here?" The Beloved named Allie made an aborted gesture. "Both Christian and I are frustrated that we can't be of help in the Akasha. Maybe we could find a way to get him in there? He's absolutely deadly with a sword."

"Is he?" Parisi turned to examine the Dark One.

He also bowed to her, no doubt sensing the power wrapped around Parisi. "A two-handed sword has long been my weapon of choice."

"I like you," Parisi told him. "You have sound weapon preferences. Are we ready to enter the Hour?"

"We will be as soon as—ah, there she is."

"Jenna!" Allie exclaimed as the Weaver Sally had ordered hurried around the side of the toilet block. "What … I'm not sure I understand what is going on. Are you going to try to portal your way into the Hour?"

"Jenna, what a pleasure to see you again. Let me introduce you." Aisling ran through the introductions of Parisi and Mabel before turning to Sally. "You can't portal into the Akasha, can you? At least … no one ever told me it was possible."

"Oh, it's not," Jenna told them all with a bright smile. "Imagine the Weaver abuse that would go on should we be able to zap people out of the impossible-to-leave Akasha."

"Jim's left it," Aisling said with obvious pride.

"Yup," the demon answered. "Got the Hashmallim to let me out."

Everyone but Sally stared at the demon in astonishment. She had a faint memory of a report Terrin had written stating that he'd finally dealt with Titania, who had been unjustly banished by the cheating Oberon, but that he'd had to involve a demon to pull it off. Her respect for what she termed her better half—she'd never made any bones about the fact that he was definitely the more valuable of the two of them—went up another notch.

"That's ... how did you do that?" Jenna asked.

"Sang 'My Humps' to them for a couple of days straight," Jim admitted with a twist of its lips. "Almost went mad doing it, but I had a fairy who wanted revenge on her ex, so I had to do what I had to do. Are we going in? Because it's almost dinnertime, and my coat goes to Abaddon in a basket if I don't eat in a timely manner."

"Right, remember how I told you that you are not to bother people with trivial talk? This is a perfect example of that. So stick to answering questions, or offering information if it can help. Yes. It's an official order. Speaking of that, do I need to give anyone temporary demon lord powers over Jim? I talked to Nora a few minutes ago, and she wasn't sure if Jim would be OK in the Hour if it didn't have someone who could directly give it orders."

"It's not like it's Abaddon," Jim said with a roll of its eyes.

"It should be fine so far as I know, but I'm happy to take charge of it for you, if you would like," Sally said, smiling at the demon.

It backed up a step.

"I think I'll pass if it's not necessary," Aisling said, her eyes big as her gaze skittered away from Sally. "But I'm still confused about how you're getting into the Hour if Jenna isn't going to open a portal."

"We're going to blip," Jenna answered, then turned to face the back of the toilet block. She shook out her hands, and lowered her head to focus. Sally felt another prickle of static on her arms, but this feeling was different. It lacked the punch of dread that was bound to dark power. "I just need to charge up for a minute."

"What's a blip?" Sally heard Allie ask Christian.

"I'd like to know the answer to that, as well," Gabriel replied. The others nodded.

Jenna ignored them while she gathered power, so Sally figured she'd better do the explanation. "Jenna is a unique Weaver in that she can not only open a portal to a different location and time—she can also blip, which I believe is her word for translocating short distances."

"Translocating?" Aisling's brows furrowed. "Isn't that the same thing as opening up a portal for us?"

"No. Jenna's blips can only go a short distance. But they work through obstacles such as walls." Sally glanced at Jenna, who was humming softly to herself. The sense of drawing in the air, of static electricity pulled from around them, made her feel as if she were standing in a lightning storm.

"But ... how does that help ... oh." Aisling blinked a couple of times.

"Wow," May said at the same time.

"What am I missing?" Mabel asked, glancing around the group. "I don't need a blip to take Parisi to the Hour. All she has to do is request it of me, and I can take her there."

"I believe the idea is that Jenna can use her abilities to transport Jim and Sally directly into the Hour," Gabriel explained.

Sally nodded. "Like I said, Jenna can blip short distances. Right through walls of buildings. Or in this case, the barrier that separates the Hour from the mortal world. That should get demon Jim and me inside, while Mabel takes Parisi in through more conventional methods."

"OK, that's impressive," Aisling said.

"And handy," Allie agreed. "I wish the vamps could do something like that."

Christian gave her a long-suffering look before wrapping an arm around her waist.

"OK, I'm ready. We have to do this quickly, because the structure of the Hour barrier is fluctuating every half minute or so, which means I lose it."

Jim looked at Parisi. "I think we're a go now."

"Hmm?" Parisi seemed to be daydreaming and blinked a few times before saying, "Ah, just so. Reaper, it is my desire and request that you take me to the Thirteenth Hour. Preferably close to where the others are located."

"One entrance to the worst place in the underworld coming up," Mabel said cheerfully, and holding her moonstone pendant, she winked at Jim before the two of them disappeared into nothing.

Jenna gave a nod, her gaze still on the back of the toilet block. "And now it's our turn. If everyone would snuggle up next to me, I'll count to three; then you'll hopefully blip in."

"You're not going with them?" Aisling asked Jenna as Jim and Sally scooted close to her. The Weaver stood with her head bowed and her arms outstretched, palms facing the building.

"Can't." Jenna's gaze remained fixed on the wall before her. "No Weavers allowed unless cursed there. Ready?"

Sally put one hand on Jim's collar, the other on Jenna's arm, and braced herself for the translocation.

There was a moment's feeling of all her atoms separating, then slamming back together in a manner that left her momentarily without breath.

Jim staggered forward, directly into a figure that resolved itself into Mabel, who collapsed. Sally was relieved to see both women, although she noted that even

Parisi took two steps forward before she stumbled and went down to her knees.

Around them, a heavy silence fell. "It's almost sticky," Sally said without thinking, glancing around.

"What ... holy shitsnacks, I feel like I slammed into a freight train. ... What feels sticky? And why has this guiding affected me like this? I've never been touched by the underworld before," Mabel asked as she got to a sitting position, weaving slightly.

"I was talking about the silence. As for your discomfort, it's most likely the security built into the Hour perimeter. I believe I shall sit down for a moment to gather myself. The Carrie Fay Academy of Shiny Hair and Uplifted Tatas has strong things to say about cavorting around without being gathered." She sat on a smooth reddish-brown rock bench and took stock of the situation.

"It would appear we're in some sort of prison. I guess that makes sense, although I wouldn't think it was necessary, given the protection woven into the Hour itself," Mabel said, dragging herself over to plop down on a stone stair.

"It looks like a crypt to me," Jim said, wobbling for a few steps. "Smells like one, too."

Sally took a few discreet sniffs. "I can smell nothing but damp, although I agree the general vibe given off is that of abandoned, haunted crypt. One with large spiders, velociraptors, and giant chupacabras."

Parisi had made it over to one of the walls, and Sally realized that what she'd thought of as an antechamber or a small reception room was actually the landing of a stairway that led downward, into the dank, damp earth. The doorways were suitably Gothic in their arches, while occasional wall alcoves held dismally burning torches, from which an acrid gray smoke emitted, curling its way to a ceiling so high, it was a vague haze above them.

Despite the low level of light, Sally realized that what she had first thought were mildew stains on the stone were actually some form of writing. She rose and moved to Parisi's side, her eyes narrowing on the stone wall facing them. "I am not familiar with this language," she said absently.

"It is Sibli," Parisi said, her gaze scanning the wall. "Used many millennia ago by the protomages, and spelled with prohibitions. These symbols here, though, are different."

Sally studied them. "I do not remember Sibli, but a few of the runes look familiar."

"Sibli is an ancient language," Parisi said, trailing a finger along the carved stone as she moved down the wall toward the sunken stairs. "It was old when I was young."

"When was that?" Jim asked, coming over to look at the wall. It didn't look impressed.

Parisi gave it a little smile. "Well before you, demon."

"Well, yeah. I mean, you are my mom," Jim answered.

Sally wasn't at all surprised when Parisi did not acknowledge the statement. She had an air about her that warned she had been in the Beyond for many hundreds of years, and thus had probably lost touch with her life in the mortal world. "These runes are about four thousand years old, I believe. It looks to me like it's a prophecy."

"It is," Parisi said, dusting her hand on her hip before starting toward the stairs. "One that warns that violation of this Hour will result in the breaking of the Otherworld. Shall we proceed? Much as I am enjoying my time in your reality, I cannot be away from my home for long lest Don Diego get it into his head that he leads the other defenders in their daily fitness."

Jim and Mabel looked at Sally. "Should we be worried about potentially breaking the entire Otherworld?" Mabel asked.

"I'm not," Sally answered. "I don't see why you should want to do so, but you do you. And yes, it's probably best we get moving before the Hashmallim figure out where we are. Let me see. … If I remember the map Terrin had of the Hour, the lake should be down the stairs in a subcellar."

Sally made a few mental notes about their trip through the maze that made up the Thirteenth Hour. Although she remembered Terrin's map, it had been fairly bare of details, so it took her a few tries before they emerged into a cavern filled with blackness and the gentle plop of wetness dripping to the floor.

"Jim, I believe it's time to bring out those things I gave you to carry," Sally said, her hands on her hips as she studied the unmoving black water. She had to admit that just looking at it gave her an uneasy feeling, and for a moment, she considered tapping into the joint power that she and Terrin shared, but gave a headshake at that temptation.

"Gotcha." Jim shimmied out of the Hello Kitty backpack it wore, and opened it before spilling out the contents on the dirt floor.

"Light first, I think," Sally said, handing four camping lanterns to Mabel. "If you could place them along the shore. I have waterproof headlamps for those of you going into the water."

"You're not coming with us?" Jim asked her, its brows furrowed.

"I can't. I shouldn't be here to begin with, but I couldn't resist seeing Desislav again. You'll have to do the heavy lifting, I'm afraid. There are waterproof headlamps for both of you. Oh yes, the orange air canisters are really mini breathing devices. I got them in the Seychelles. Really quite handy things to have. You just pop that end into your mouth, and you'll have ten minutes of air."

"Why didn't I think to have Aisling get me a wet suit when she got Parisi hers?" Jim asked as it snuffled the breathing tube. Parisi quickly stripped down to her skivvies before donning a black-and-yellow wet suit. "My coat is going to dry all funky, I just know it."

"I have about an hour left. I hate to hurry you, but …" Mabel let her sentence trail off, and moved back to the stairs to wait.

Sally showed Parisi how to use the breathing device, then turned to Jim. She strapped onto him first a headlamp, then the breathing device before turning on the flow of air. It bobbed its head a few times in an indication it could breathe before it followed Parisi into the inky water.

"That water really does not look right," Sally murmured to herself as the pair disappeared under the water, the plume of Jim's tail the last thing she saw.

"How is water not right?" Mabel asked, looking up from her phone.

"It's … just wrong. But so fitting with the place, don't you think? Whoever designed it deserves an award." Sally looked around with approval for whoever was in charge of the Hour's appearance. "I mean, if you're going to make a place of ultimate suffering inside a place known for its endless torment, you're going to need it to be something special. And this is definitely out of the norm."

Mabel stared at her in obvious horror. "Are you insane? This is the hellish hell version of the ultimate hell, and you admire the decor?"

"Of course. Even evil needs recognition." Sally smiled at the reaper, but Mabel continued to look horrified and scooted a bit farther away.

Sally sighed to herself and made a mental note to tell Terrin about the latest drama with the dragons. She had a feeling he would be more than a little peeved with her, but she always found that to be one of his charms, and settled in to wait for the submariners to return.

THIRTEEN
Diary of Effrijim, Demon Sixth Class

As if it's not hard enough to know that your own mom doesn't recognize you—although to be fair, I didn't recognize her, either, not that I would because she left a couple of days after I was born—but then you find out your dad was one of the most feared beings in the history of the Otherworld, and it kinda wallops you.

I knew I had to help my mom even if she didn't remember me because she'd been stuck in the Beyond for so long, but man alive, I never thought I'd go scuba diving to do it. And yet, as I dove under the black—and surprisingly warm—water, the headlight illuminating a few yards in front of us, I had no idea just what we'd find.

Let me tell you what we found—a whole crap ton of scary.

We didn't see the bodies until we swam down for half a minute; then all of a sudden Parisi's headlight caught the foot of a body floating upside down. It was enough to give me the willies, although that ramped up when, as I swam closer to the body, it twisted, the bound hands flailing as the man turned to face me. He opened his mouth in what was probably a scream and tried to grab at me in a scissor move with his legs.

He just got one of his legs around my torso before I could move away, and was pulling me toward him, his hold like iron, when all of a sudden I was jerked backward, and Parisi was there, waving her sword at the guy. He continued to silent scream at us, and at a gesture from her, I followed really close to her as we swam forward another ten yards or so before she suddenly pointed upward and started to ascend.

I was right on her heels, and when we broke the surface of the water, I made it to the shore in record dog-paddling time.

"Fires of Abaddon," I said, coughing a little at a near intake of water into my lungs as I spat out the breathing-device mouthpiece. "That was the creepiest thing I've ever seen in my life, and I worked in Abaddon for more than four hundred years."

"So the Upside-Down Sinners thing wasn't just an atmospheric name?" Mabel asked as Parisi likewise took off her breathing thing and sank down onto the floor, staring at nothing.

"Yeah," I answered, and looked at Sally, trying to tell if she knew what was in the lake. On the whole, I had a feeling she did, even if she hadn't ever seen it for herself. "It looks like they're chained by their hands to the floor. I don't know how many there are, but one of them tried to grab me with his legs, so we got out of there."

"I believe the last count is one thousand three hundred twenty-seven sinners," Sally said, pursing her lips as I shook off the water that was trying to get through my undercoat.

"Jeezumcrow," Mabel murmured, her eyes huge.

"That's not the worst." I wondered if I had cell reception in the Hour. I thought not, but I had a sudden urge to call Aisling and tell her a dead guy grabbed me, but that my mom had saved me. "They're alive down there. Just floating, but they can scream. Kind of. At least, I think that was a scream. What do you think?" I asked the last bit of Parisi, who gave a little shudder and looked up.

"Yes. They are very much alive. I didn't realize there were so many of them. I don't know what this Destroyer person looks like. I assume you don't know, either?" she asked me.

"Nope." We both turned to Sally.

"I'm sorry, I can't go in the lake. That's a hard-line no," she told us, but, after a moment's thought, added, "He is a demigod, though. Parisi, you should be able to feel the power surrounding him. That's what I'd suggest you look for ... someone who feels like dark power. Lots of it."

She didn't look thrilled with the idea, but I'll give my mom this: she held to her promises. She stood up and picked up my breathing apparatus, strapping it onto my head. "I'll do my best, although this is not at all the sort of saving I had imagined. I normally fight body to body with swords and daggers and my lovely pair of pearl-handled ladies' beheading axes. I quite like the axes."

"As do I. There's nothing more satisfying than a really well-balanced beheading axe, especially if you get a good swing going, but honestly, you don't have anything to worry about the lack of physical combat," Sally said with the tiniest of smiles. "You'll have more than enough action trying to get Desi out of here. And speaking of that, I'd like to be done before Sasha tattles to Terrin that we're actually in the Hour at this moment, so onward, *mes braves!*"

"If I don't come back up, tell Ash to give me a half hour to get the perfect Newfie form in mind before she summons me," I told Sally.

She narrowed her eyes at me. "Have you thought of a form a little more useful?"

"Like anything could beat this one?" I asked, and gave another shake that had her sputtering rude things in French, but I paid her no mind as I followed Parisi back into the unpleasant lake.

This time, Parisi held out one of the lanterns she'd snagged on her way back into the water, and swam down with it held out in front of her like a beacon.

It revealed row upon row of bodies, long chains from their hands descending into the depths. I have to admit, for a few seconds, I was doubting the wisdom of trying to find my dad, but before I could figure out how to convey that to Parisi, she swam onward, her sword held in one hand, and the lantern in the other.

I figure it had to be about at the end of our ten minutes of air when we hit a part of the lake that was cold. Like, intensely cold. The sort of cold that even the thickest of Newfie coats won't keep out. Parisi gestured, and dove even deeper until we could see a metal grid on the lake bottom, from which all the sinners' chains ascended.

A black shape loomed before us. Parisi hesitated for a moment, turning her head to look at me. I didn't know what she wanted, so I just nodded and hoped that if something really bad was in what looked a whole lot like a black shroud, I'd have enough time to get my replacement form just right.

And then she reached out, tearing the fabric off the

body that hung there so silent, encased in cold that I could start to feel freeze my body.

The body twisted around to face us. I couldn't see much other than he had long black hair, dark eyes, and an expression that made my stomach want to flip-flop. He stared at Parisi for a moment, then arched back, his legs kicking out while he tried to use his shackled hands to grab her. She jerked back out of his reach, dropping the lantern in the process. It settled to the ground beneath us.

I noticed that the mini oxygen tank was starting to frost. My body was definitely freezing, my heart rate slowing down to the point where it was hard to see or even think.

And that's when I saw the shadow emerge from the right. One minute we were a few yards away from the man in the black shroud, who continued to struggle and thrash, his face contorted, and the next, three boggarts were on us, one of them stabbing at my side with a nasty dagger.

I don't know how Parisi fights on land, but submerged in a lake filled with 1,300 sinners, she was the best I'd ever seen.

The second the dagger stabbed into my side, Parisi was there, kicking at the boggart before doing a very slow twirl to swing her sword at the two who were closing in on her from behind.

Green leaked out of their headless bodies, the surprised expressions on their faces enough to distract me from the fact that I could no longer feel my legs.

The third boggart took one look at Parisi and swam off. Without looking at me, she grabbed my collar and started to haul me upward.

Halfway up, the oxygen ran out.

We surfaced to a dull throbbing sound that seemed to echo through the stone itself.

Sally was pacing the shore, her hands gesticulating when she saw us. "There you are! What have you been doing down there to set off alarms?"

"Boggarts," I gasped when Parisi more or less dragged me out of the water. My legs felt completely numb, and I was having a hard time getting my lungs to take in oxygen. "Three of them guarding the dead guys, including the one who I think is my dad. Parisi killed them. I think I have frostbite on at least half of my body. Man, if I lose another toe, I'm going to be so mad. I'm missing two as it is. Minus three is just not a look I want Cecile to see."

"We have to leave now," Sally said, and for once, the look of amusement that usually lurks in her eyes was gone. She put everything into my backpack while Mabel was waiting impatiently at the entrance to the stairs up.

"But we didn't get my dad," I said when Sally tried to lift me to my feet. My legs felt like rubber and didn't want to hold my otherwise magnificent form. "He's still down there, seriously pissed."

"We don't have time for this," Sally said, and with a couple of words sent me spinning into the Akasha. The regular part of it.

I looked around at a startled troll who held a yoga mat and a large water bottle, clearly about to pass by the location where Sally had flung me.

"I really hate it when people treat me like a demon," I told the troll.

"Dude," he said in a surfer drawl, then proceeded past me.

It took a half hour before I felt my toes again, and a few minutes after that, a familiar sense of being pulled started down my back. I sat down, letting the feeling consume me.

"Jim! Are you all right? Parisi said you were freezing, and had lost some toes. Here, I have an electric blanket for you. Just sit there and let me cover you in it." My vision cleared and Aisling loomed into view, her face twisted with worry.

"I'm OK now," I said, rubbing my head on her leg as she knelt next to me, because even a demon lord needs to know you love them. "Parisi saved me, although I had no idea that Sally could banish me to the Akasha. I thought only you or a duly authorized representative of you could do that."

"I have depths," came a Southern drawl from behind me. I gave a little shiver of pleasure when the heat of the blanket soaked into my still damp coat. "Or so my current partner says. Romantic partner, not Terrin, although, come to think of it, he's made references to my naughty side more than once. But there we are."

Sally was seated on the couch in Ash and Drake's living room. Mabel was gone, but Parisi was curled up in a chair with another blanket around her. But it was her expression that had me getting to my feet and going over to nose her hand. "Hey," I said.

"I knew him." Her face was a mask of confusion, her eyes dark with pain. "I knew him, and yet, I didn't. That was him, yes? The one you want freed? He was in such torment."

"That was him," I said, giving another shiver at the memory of the despair in what had to be my dad's eyes. "How did you guys get out? I assume you had Mabel zap you out?"

"Yes," she said, then pulled the blanket up higher on her shoulders, her eyes troubled. I studied her for a moment. She looked like a Bollywood actress, with shiny black hair, dark gray eyes, and an oval face with a little cleft in her chin. I thought of my human form, and wondered about the fact that it also had a chin cleft. "The reaper took me, and Sally took herself. It matters little. I must meditate on this. I do not understand, and that disturbance will have a detrimental effect on my ability to protect."

"What happened other than you nearly froze to death?" Aisling asked, setting down in front of me a bowl of what smelled like broth.

"No meat? No veggies?" I asked her, sniffing the bowl again.

"Drink your warm broth," she said in an annoyed tone that filled me with relief. Not that I minded being pampered, but I didn't like the strain around her eyes. I slurped at the soup while Sally and Parisi gave a brief recap of our adventure.

"Boggarts," Aisling said with a near snort. "Those bastards are just evil. You think they're guards, Sally?"

"I don't know for certain, not having looked specifically into the running of the Thirteenth Hour, but yes, it was clear how they swarmed us that they were intent on stopping Parisi and Effrijim from freeing the handsome Desi."

Parisi shot a sharp glance at Sally, but almost immediately withdrew back into the confines of her blanket, her expression abstracted.

"You recognized him, though," Aisling said, turning to Parisi. "That must mean your memory is returning. That has to be a huge relief."

"No, I do not know the man. That is … I recognize something about him, but I do not *know* him. It is clear, however, he is in torment, and as a defender of those who cannot help themselves, I am obligated to release him from his prison."

"I don't know how we're going to do that with the place crawling with boggarts," I said with a faint flicker of hope. If Aisling was right, then Parisi was getting her memory back, even if it was just a little bit at a time. "We'd have to get rid of them, and I can't do that by myself."

Sally heaved a dramatic sigh and rose from the sofa. "I suppose I shall have to volunteer to distract the guards while you and Parisi rescue Desi. If Mabel is done with her phone call, we can return to the Hour. Jenna is waiting for us near the Hyde Park toilets."

"Oh, I don't know. … Is it safe for you to return so soon? Jim's form was almost destroyed by the cold," Aisling said, making me give her another fast head rub to the leg. "And Parisi seemed to be affected by it, as well."

"Affected but not damaged by it, defenders being what they are," Parisi murmured.

"If we're going to the Hour again, I'd strongly urge you to get going now rather than later. The director at my ballet is not going to be happy if I have to take more time off for an injury that has actually healed." Mabel appeared in the doorway, not looking annoyed, as I'd half expected, but somehow worried. Anxious. Almost frightened.

I wondered about that.

"Jim?" Aisling looked at me with a line between her brows. "Do you feel up to it?"

"Yeah. I mean, it's no walk in the park with burgers after, but I kinda feel like I have to help, you know?"

"I know," she said, and gathered up the stuff for my backpack.

It took a little longer than we anticipated, but an hour later, we trotted down the stone stairs to the Lake of Upside-Down Sinners.

"Fresh breathers," Sally said as I nosed the devices out of my backpack.

"Check," I said.

"Underwater flares, six."

"Check. You think those will work?"

She gave the slightest of shrugs. "If I was a guard swimming around a black lake filled with thirteen hundred sinners, I'd certainly be interested enough in strange lights to go investigate."

"Suppose so," I agreed, although a bit hesitantly. I wondered if Sally knew just how devious boggarts could be.

They were on Aisling's list of least favorite beings, because they were the size of a six-year-old child and looked like they were a million years old with twisted, hunched backs and faces that would give even an elite wrath demon nightmares.

And they were cunning. Very cunning.

"The flares are just to get their attention." Sally made a show of examined them, twirling them around her fingers in a way that made think for a moment of human form. "And when they come out of the water, I'll hit them with the flamethrower."

"What flamethrower?" I asked, looking up from nosing the pair of bolt cutters toward Parisi. She was adjusting a belt on top of her wet suit, strapping to herself her axes, scabbard, and sword.

"Didn't I tell you I found a flamethrower lying around?" Sally looked as innocent as a baby whose mom diminished into another realm a few hours after his birth. "You know how boggarts dislike fire."

"Yeah, but not the big imps they like to run around with," I said, thinking back to the previous Christmas when we were stuck in an airport.

"OK, I'm down to less than an hour before I have to leave," Mabel said, looking out of sorts with everyone. "Mysteriously appearing flamethrowers aside, please, for the love of Freed, go rescue your father."

"Who's Freed?" I couldn't help but ask.

"Maker of my favorite pointe shoes. *Vámanos*!" she answered, shooing me toward the water.

"Oh good, this has a handy intensity knob. I just know those boggarts will appreciate the maximum distance of flame. Are you ready?" Sally twirled a couple more underwater flares.

"Yes," Parisi said, snagging the bolt cutters and also tucking them into her belt. "Although I have my doubts about these snips being able to cut through the chain binding the man Desi."

"Oh, you're going to have to help them along," Sally said as she flipped a few switches on the flamethrower I one hundred percent had not seen her bring with us. "Give them some oomph."

"Oomph?" Parisi wrinkled her nose. "I do not know this oomph. Is it a spell?"

"It means you're going to have to use your power to help," I told her, eyeing the black water.

I really didn't relish going in there and possibly freezing this fabulous form, but I couldn't leave my dad down there. Not only were the vamps counting on him to deal with their big, bad, but he was my dad. It would be nice to have more family than just Aisling, Drake, and the spawns.

"Then let us proceed and relieve the poor sufferer from his torment," Parisi said with a lift of her chin as she marched into the water with a gesture toward me. "You do not wear the wet suit?"

"Naw, I'm a Newfie. I gots me a waterproof under-coat."

"Very well, then," she said with a nod. "Come along, demon Jim!"

"Aye aye, *mon capitaine*," I said, giving her a jaunty salute that she completely missed. Sally saw it, though, and smiled as she snapped two flares to mix the chemicals inside them, then tossed them into the water as I dove in.

This time, we stayed close to the surface, where none of the dead sinners could grab at us. It wasn't until we hit that freezing cold corner that we dove down into a darkness that seemed to be made up of dense, dark nothingness. Cold nothingness.

I ignored the burning of my ears and toes as the cold immediately seeped into them, and focused on helping Parisi as she approached the man around whom there still remained tattered bits of the black shroud. He twisted around as we approached, his legs kicking wildly.

Dimly, in the distance, I heard some sort of an air horn sound; then the top of the water was lit up like someone was letting off fireworks right above the surface.

That'll get the boggarts' attention, I mused as Parisi deftly avoided being kicked or captured by Desi's wild legs, and sank down to the bottom, where she started to cut at the manacles.

She kicked around a couple of times, which I assumed was her getting her oomph on, and by the dim light of my headlamp, I saw one of the shackles drop. The instant it fell free, Desi grabbed Parisi by the front of her wet suit. I dove toward him, knocking his hand away and baring my teeth, but before I could do more, the black shapes were on us again.

Sally's distraction clearly failed, but the two attacking boggarts didn't last long. I bit one hard on the arm, spitting out the nasty blackish-green blood that filled my mouth. Parisi dual-wielded her beheading axes and put them to use. She stared at Desi, who was struggling to release his still-bound hand, but the booming noise we'd heard before—which Sally had said was an ancient alarm system intended on drawing more guards to the area—was making the water reverberate, so we swam upward again.

We were attacked three more times as we made our way to the edge of the lake, brilliant flashes of flame momentarily lighting up the entire area, making the surface of the water dance with its reflected glow.

Parisi beheaded the last boggart that had followed us, leaving us to drag our half-frozen selves out of the water.

Sally stood with one hand on her hip, surrounded by a pile of blackened and burned boggarts.

"We must leave now! Effrijim!" Sally said, slipping the flamethrower's strap across her chest.

"I know, I know. Mabel takes Parisi out, and you zap me back to the Akasha. Please tell Ash not to wait so long this time. It's cold with wet fur."

Fifteen minutes later, I was snuggled up with the same electric blanket, and another bowl of boring broth in front of me. "At least it's hot," I said as I sipped at it, wondering if my toes would ever be the same.

FOURTEEN
Parisi

The dragons were having a discussion. It was useless, but I've ever believed in allowing people to make their own choices, whether for good or ill, without input from me unless I was specifically asked.

The dragons did not ask.

"We need to get Parisi and Jim some protection while Parisi is undoing Desi's shackles," the one named Aisling said, looking to the other dragons present for agreement.

"I don't know how we can pull that off," May, mate of the silver wyvern, said with a look of doubt toward Jim. "Sally, can you banish Gabriel and me to the Akasha like you do Jim?"

"You are not a demon," she said with a slight shake of her head.

"What does that have to do with the Akasha?" Aisling asked. "Anyone can be sent to it, not just demons."

"In the normal course of events, yes, but trying to banish anyone from what is already a prison of banishment is extremely difficult. I'll be honest with you, sugar—the only reason I can banish the demon Jim is because of my time as a demon lord. I have just enough powers left from that to be able to send a demon wherever I want."

"What about Finch?" the Dark One's mate asked, turning to him. "This place is an Hour, and you said all the leaders of the Hours could visit each other. Could we get Finch in on the action that way?"

"I am not sure," Christian answered, rubbing his chin. Something about the gesture made my stomach tighten ... and not in a good way. "I will ask him if he'd be able to leave it should he be able to travel there."

They discussed that point for a while, then switched to other options, including bribing the Hashmallim, and ways Sally might be able to help without bringing down the wrath of the Court upon her head. I let them carry on while I pinpointed the feelings I'd felt while trying to free the prisoner Desislav.

Why did he feel familiar, and yet also was surrounded by so much rage that it turned the very water cold around him? I did not know rageful people. But the way his dark hair moved around his head ... I shook my own head at the nonsensical idea that I knew him. The others might be confused about that, but I was not.

I was a Defender of the Blood, nothing more. The others were clearly mistaken. Still, I had things to do back at my home, and for that reason, I interrupted the cyclical nature of their discussion. "I don't need someone to protect me while I am freeing the prisoner Desislav; I need someone to attack the boggarts before we enter the water."

The silence that followed was pleasing.

"The best offense is a good defense," Aisling said slowly, looking at the Dark One and dragons. "Why didn't we think of that? Of course it would be easier to go in and blast out the boggarts before you finish breaking Jim's dad free. But … can you do that by yourself?"

I thought for a moment. "No," I finally admitted. "I will need another."

"Dude. Like I'm made of mashed potatoes?" the demon dog asked. "I'm here to help save my dad, even if it means I lose my fabulous form killing boggarts."

"No one is asking you to lose your form," Aisling told it, patting it on the side.

I gave it another look, planning on making a pointed comment about how it couldn't even hold a weapon, but its eyes … its eyes seemed to pluck at my insides in a way that was wholly unfamiliar to me.

I thought of how it had looked when it stood before me in man form. Again, there was something about the eyes, and the shape of the face. It was as if a thought was nudging me from a very long distance, a prod so gentle I wasn't sure if it was really there or not. Rather than telling the demon that it was at best useless, and worse a liability that I'd have to protect while dealing with the attackers, the words that spilled from my mouth were, "Your aid is welcome, although the number of boggarts demands a third person, preferably one with a bladed weapon."

"Present!" a man's voice came from Aisling's laptop. "It's been a few months since I've had to use my sword, but I will gladly accompany you to the Hour."

"But can you go to the Hour, Finch?" Allie asked, leaning forward to see the screen better. "Christian wasn't sure if you could get out even if you can travel to it."

"I checked with the former steward who ran this Hour—and did an exceptionally good job at it, so much so that Tatiana and I are trying to lure him back into the job—and he said that being the lord of an Hour gives me the ability to enter and exit *any* Hour," Finch answered.

"Thank all the little imps for that," Sally said, her gaze on me for a few seconds. I felt the impact of her gaze and lifted my head to study her. Power was woven around her in varying bands, manifesting itself as a variety of colors ranging from pale pink to a deep maroon, lime green, and a soft yellow. She also bore a symbol on her brow, one I saw every time I looked in the mirror.

Unable to keep from asking, I leaned down and asked the demon Jim, "Can you see the symbol on my head?"

"The one from the Court?" It tipped its head to the side, giving me a long side-eye. "Yeah. It's the same one that Sally has."

I touched my forehead, wondering about that. I had never questioned the symbol, but now I wondered if perhaps some of my past might not have been erased by my time in the Beyond.

"But that's folly," I said softly, giving a mental head-shake. "I've only been in there a short time."

"Try sixteen hundred years," Jim said, now watching me carefully. "That's when I was born."

"I would know if I had a child," I told the demon.

"Would you, though?" it asked, and I couldn't find an answer.

"It's just a damned shame we can't get a couple of dragons in the place, too," Aisling said, kicking at a pillow that had fallen off a couch.

"Well, you can't," Sally said as she stood up and stretched. "Not unless they have got some demon in them that I could use to get a grip in order to send them to the Akasha. Shall we reconvene tomorrow? Jenna said she'd be available then, and assuming we can drag Mabel away from her dance studio, we can give it another try with the handsome Finch."

"The *taken* handsome Finch," his mate corrected, giving the screen a gimlet look.

"Wait, wait, wait," Aisling said when Sally started moving toward the door. "You said we could get a dragon into the Hour if he was partially a demon, yes?"

"Oooh," Jim said, giving a low whistle. "Now, that's an idea."

"There are only three dragon hunters in existence," Sally told Aisling. "If that's what you're thinking of."

Aisling smiled. "There may have been three, but now there's five, and one of the two is in town, and according to what Drake said, he's chock-full of demonic dark power. That was his shtick before he and his twin were balanced so now they both have dragon and demon powers."

"Interesting," Sally said with slightly narrowed eyes as she watched Aisling tapping furiously on her phone. "I hadn't heard about this, but admittedly, my contact with dragonkin is normally limited to May and her manly thighed Gabriel. Very well, if you have a dragon hunter on tap, I should be able to throw him into the Akasha with Jim once we are finished."

"Gee, thanks," the demon said, but I had to admit it looked a lot more cheerful than a few minutes before.

"Two extra fighters should be sufficient, but I cannot stay another day," I announced, standing up. I made a snap decision not because I wanted to return home so badly, but because of the unsettled feeling I had the more time I spent around the demon Jim. Also, the expression on the prisoner's face when he'd seen me haunted my memory. It had gone from torment to intense joy to fear and dread and fury unlike anything I'd felt. "So either we do this now, or I'm afraid you'll have to find someone else to free Desislav."

Silence filled the room. The dragon and the Dark Ones exchanged glances; then Aisling said, "I guess we can rally everyone now for a third try. Er … Finch …"

"I'll get ready and meet you just inside the entrance of the Hour. It shouldn't take me longer than thirty minutes," Finch answered, nodding when the other Dark One spoke in an old form of an Eastern European language before ending the video call.

I recognized the language from … my brain seemed to skitter away from the name I was seeking. I worried for a few minutes about that, but by the time I had my thoughts under control again, the others were preparing to return to the Hour.

"If you don't mind, I'll guide you from here rather than going all the way out to Hyde Park," Reaper Mabel told me twenty-seven minutes later, after she (somewhat wearily) greeted everyone as they were leaving. "We can wait at the antechamber, if you all like."

"That is agreeable to me," I told her, then added, "I wish to be taken to the Thirteenth Hour."

"Your wish is my command," she answered with a wry twist of her lips, and then the feeling of being turned inside out claimed me as we entered the Hour.

"I've got to deal with a potential disaster at work," Mabel told me, holding up her phone. "If you don't mind, I'll go hunker down in the corner and try to put out the fires."

"I thought you were a dancer?" I asked.

"I am. But that's my mortal-world job. I also work for …" Her words trailed off as she gestured vaguely.

I waited for her to finish, but she simply gave me a somewhat lame smile and plopped herself down on a rock, her phone in hand.

I was about to go dip into the water and see if any boggarts were patrolling—which I thought they might do after our two breaches of their lake—but just then a Dark One marched down the stairs and greeted us.

"Hello again. It's a pleasure to see you both in person. I'm Finch Dante, in case you missed the introductions on the Zoom call. Ah, so this is the infamous Lake of Upside-Down Sinners. I must make notes for my Beloved, Tatiana. She is quite interested in all sorts of oddities and curiosities, and this certainly place definitely qualifies as one." The Dark One was suitable bulky and tall enough to reassure me he'd be able to handle himself in a fight, although I noted his sword was not two-handed.

"Thank you for helping," I said politely, my gaze still on the sword.

"I'm more than happy to do what I can to assist in putting our missing thane back into my Hour," he responded, then shot me a curious look. "Is there something about me that is bothering you?"

"Yes," I said, believing in being forthright whenever possible. "Your sword."

He pulled it from where it hung at his side. "What's wrong with it?"

"It's one-handed. A two-handed sword is usually more effective when beheading boggarts," I pointed out, drawing from my back my own sword. "This is Mina, light of the night sky. You'll notice it's two-handed. All Defenders of the Blood carry such swords."

"But I am not a Defender of the Blood," he pointed out, but examined the sword when I held it out for his approval. "That said, it is a lovely sword. Does the name have a meaning?"

"Yes, of course. All swords that bear a name have a reason for such. In this case, it was spelled by Mina, who was …" I stopped, my memory once again shying away from pulling forth the information I wanted. "She was … she spelled the blade," I repeated, troubled by the fact that I couldn't remember.

"Just so. I'm sure it's highly effective in your hands, but I am not so lucky as to have more than single-handed swords. This one was my father's favorite, and I find it works well with me."

"By the living darkness, I think you've killed me," came a voice from behind Finch. It had an Irish lilt to it, but was decidedly male.

"You're such a big baby. What's a little translocation to a deadly dragon hunter?" The woman who spoke trotted down the stairs. She had an odd twisted hairstyle that looked like blobs on the top of her head, but there was a brightness about her that was unfamiliar to me, although I thought she might be some sort of sprite.

She stopped when she saw me, and then made a deep bow. "Goodness, a Sovereign. I had no idea that you were the warrior Hunter said needed some help. Now I'm glad I agreed to help him one last time."

"Fires of Abaddon," Jim gasped as it literally tumbled down the last few stairs. "The Weaver's blipping gets worse every time. Are all my toes present?"

"This is Clover," the dragon named Hunter said by way of an introduction. "She is my esprit."

"*Was* your esprit. I'm divorcing you because you are not boyfriend material," the almost-sprite snapped back.

"I never told you that I was," he argued. "I explained to you when you signed on to power my élan vital that I wasn't a one-woman sort of man. I never have been, and I never will be."

A snorting sound came from the corner of the antechamber.

Hunter glanced toward Mabel. "Pardon?"

"Nothing," she said without looking up from where she was continuing to tap on her phone. "I just snorted derisively."

"And you are … ?" he asked, his arms crossed as he glared at her.

"Not really any of your business," she said, pursing her lips as she continued to type on the phone. "Not unless you are ready to go to the afterlife."

"You must be the reaper," he said, his gaze lingering on her.

"Are we ready?" Sally asked, dumping the contents of Jim's backpack on the ground. "I hope this is going to be enough mini-breathers. The shop where I get them is now sold out. Also, I had to guess on wet suit sizes, so no complaints if they don't fit well."

The next few minutes were spent in everyone stripping down to don the wet suits, although both the Dark One and the dragon hunter protested that they needed no such thing.

"You say that now, but when your toes drop off, you're gonna be sorry," Jim told them.

"The area where the prisoner is being held is icy to the point of disabling," I said, and adjusted my sword so I could reach it easier.

"Shall we?" Hunter asked the sprite.

"OK, but this is the last time. You're just going to have to convince another esprit to take over, because

Sasha says I can work for her for a bit while I decide what I want to do."

He bowed and held out his sword—two-handed, and beautifully scribed and gemmed—and she shrank down into a ball of brilliant yellow light that bobbed down the length of the sword before it settled into an empty socket at the cross guard.

I led the way, and although obviously no one could speak while we were underwater, I felt the shock and surprise in the two men as we swam deeper and deeper, weaving our way through the bodies that lunged and grabbed at us.

By the time the cold started to creep around us, warning we were near the prisoner Desislav's confinement location, the booming of the ancient siren could be heard. I kicked forward, spotting the chain … but no body was attached to it.

Jim flailed for a moment in an obvious attempt to express its disbelief in what it was seeing. I knew just how it felt. Despite the cold that started to freeze the blood in my veins, I dove deeper until I could touch one of the empty shackles that rested on the floor of the lake.

Pain seared through my hand, causing me to jerk back. I felt a disturbance behind me, and spun as quickly as I could to see a handful of boggarts attacking both Hunter and Finch.

By the time I had my sword out and swam up to dispatch as many boggarts as I could, the men had the five boggarts floating off without their heads, the nasty blackish-green blood snaking toward us in insidious tendrils. I pointed upward and the men nodded. We swam up and, with slowed movements, dragged our frozen selves out of the water.

"That's … holy shit, that was cold," Hunter said, his pale green eyes looking stark. "I see why you recommended the wet suits. But … where was this demigod?"

"Gone," I said, sitting down on a step, waiting for my body to stop freezing and start to run as normal. "I don't know how, but I suspect with how twisted the second manacle was, the curses woven into it depended on both pieces binding him."

"Desi isn't there?" Sally leaped back when Jim shook itself in a manner that sprayed her with water, and looked momentarily horrified before her expression smoothed out to one of mild interest. "He couldn't have escaped the Hour, though. Not on his own. Someone would have told me if he—"

An alarm on her phone remarkably like the one that still echoed in the chamber sounded, and she glanced at it before smiling broadly. "Well, how do you like that? Evidently, Desi has broken free of his bindings and is loose in the Hour. Hashmallim and more boggarts have been dispatched to find him."

"That's just wrong," I said, feeling more myself now that my hand had stopped burning where it had touched the shackle. I couldn't imagine what it had been like to have that clapped to my wrist for more than a thousand years. No wonder the poor man looked so tormented. I had a strong urge to take him into my arms and soothe him like I would an injured animal, but shook that impulse away as foolishness brought on by the circumstances. "No one deserves that sort of punishment."

The sound of running feet on the stone stairs leading to the lake filled our room, and it was with an audible groan that Hunter rose from where he'd collapsed on the floor. "Why do attackers never give you the chance to catch your breath before they strike again?"

Despite his complaint, I approved of the stance he took at one side of the stairs, while the Dark One did likewise. I noted he had picked up one of the morning stars previously wielded by a boggart, and was pleased when he moved into place opposite Hunter.

I hefted my own sword and bowed my head in prayer to the mother sun and father moon, asking them for the strength I needed in order to defeat my foes.

They boiled down the stairs in a mass of green, black, and gray bodies, the shadows of their misshapen forms oddly disconcerting as they flickered on the walls.

"Take off their heads," Finch yelled as he swung first his sword, then the morning star, handily taking down two of the lead boggarts, while Hunter's sword flashed in the light of the lanterns, the runes on it glowing with a brilliant gold light. "They're hardier than you think if you don't take their heads."

As more and more boggarts poured down the stairs, I glanced behind me to make sure that Sally and Mabel were safely out of the way. Sally stood in front of Mabel, her hands at her sides, but the bands of power that were woven around her were almost flickering with leashed energy. I decided that she could more than take care of herself and the reaper, and turned back just as three boggarts that had raced past the fighting forms of Hunter and Finch leaped toward where Jim stood next to me.

I smiled, brief memories of battles in the past lighting up my mind, and raised my sword.

FIFTEEN
Diary of Effrijim, Demon Sixth Class

"To the left! No, your other left! No, sorry, my bad, your first left was right. I mean left. The left is the right left … ACK!" I didn't know there were as many boggarts in the world as came pouring down the stairs and into the chamber containing the Lake of Upside-Down Sinners, but there was a metric butt-ton of them, and they were all heading straight for us.

"You're not—gah!" Parisi spun around, her sword slicing through the air, a couple of boggart necks, and two boggart arms. "You are not helping with bad directions."

I lunged at the boggart that was bearing down on her, since she was twirling and twisting and leaping through the air as she fought. Ahead of us, Hunter and Finch were paring down the waves of boggarts, but about half of them slipped through to where Parisi and I were the next defense.

Behind us, I could hear Sally warning Mabel, "Be ready to get Parisi out of here the second we have these boggarts under control."

"All right," Mabel answered. I glanced behind as I bit deep onto a boggart's leg, its nasty blood filling my mouth with the taste of rotted vegetation, ignoring its screams and attempts to beat me on the head. I must have severed something important, because the boggart went down in a cloud of oaths and tried to crawl away as I spat out the nasty taste. "But … I don't want to tell you what to do, but shouldn't you be helping them? I'm a dancer, not a fighter, but you're a former Sovereign."

"Sugar, do you honestly believe if there was any way I could wade into battle and open a can of whup-ass on those boggarts, I wouldn't do so? Alas, the Court has very strong opinions about former Sovereigns dismantling the security they put in place," Sally answered, handily sidestepping when the crawling boggart tried to reach for her. She kicked it in the leg I'd bitten, which left it curling up and howling in pain. She caught me staring and smiled a smile that made my hackles rise involuntarily. "A little kick between friends is fine, though."

Parisi had been busy while I was distracted, because when I turned back to help her—although I gotta admit, my mom had it going on when it came to dispatching boggarts—there was a smallish mound of green-oozing bodies to her left. "Way to go, Mom. Can I call you Mom?" I asked.

"No," she said, screaming something wordless when six boggarts with arms linked mowed down both Finch and Hunter. The latter was up on his feet immediately, while Finch appeared to have gotten in the way of one of the boggarts' swords, because when he got to his knees, I could see the blade coming out of his back.

Finch looked down at himself as he staggered to his feet. The hilt of the sword poked out of his stomach. "You bastard! Tatiana is going to tut at me, since I swore to her I wouldn't get harmed, and I hate making her tut over something so ridiculous. Have that, you filth!"

Heads went rolling down to the water, where they slipped into the lake with a whispered splash, bodies flopped onto the ground, and the stone floor become as slippery as a skating rink by the time the flow of boggarts had slowed to a mere dribble.

I picked up one of the small knives that had dropped, and, clamping it firmly with my teeth, attacked a boggart that was rushing toward Parisi. "I think this is the last of them," I said around the hilt of the knife. "We should be good now."

"Famous last words," I heard Sally say as an uncanny silence filled the room. Well, silent except for the panting and heaving of everyone who'd just battled what seemed like an entire battalion of boggarts.

"What—" I started to say, then felt it.

"What is this strangeness?" Parisi asked, ignoring Finch's strangled scream when Hunter, without warning him, whipped the sword out from where it pierced the vampire. She was panting heavily, sweat making her face red and shiny as she looked around. "What is this feeling?"

"Oh no," I said, the feeling of dread and absolute wrongness growing stronger with each passing second. "Don't tell me they can come here?"

The last was asked of Sally, who tried to smile, but it came out strained. There was something about her eyes that I didn't like, a worried light that had me regretting everything I'd ever eaten. And I've eaten a lot of things.

"I'm afraid they can. They are the gaolers of the Akasha, and this is technically part of the Akasha."

"Who are you talking about?" Parisi asked again. "And why do I feel like I am covered in honey and a herd of biting ants is heading my way?"

"I don't think ants make a herd—" I started to say, but just then, darkness settled at the top of the stairs and started to ooze its way down.

"Hashmallim," I heard Finch say in a voice filled with amazement.

"What is—" Parisi stopped when the darkness on the stairs resolved itself into four Hashmallim, the incredibly scary, insanely powerful, inhuman beings that guarded the Akasha, and were made up of darkness and terror and a stubbornness that would do any Newfie proud. She spoke a word I didn't understand.

"Yes," Sally said, moving a step closer to Mabel. The former's expression was fairly passive, but her eyes were bright and watchful. "That is their old name, before the Court made them the guardians of the Akasha."

Parisi studied them for a second as Hunter and Finch retreated to stand a few yards in front of us. Then she rolled her shoulders, cracked her neck, and strode forward between the two men, her sword in hand. "I am Parisi of Madurai, a Defender of the Blood. You will stand aside."

"Your mom has serious balls," Mabel said softly. "I don't think I could walk up to them like that. They make me want to run away screaming while setting my hair on fire."

"Yeah, they have that effect on people," I said, then, feeling it was important to make a stand next to Parisi, shoved my way between Finch and Hunter and stopped next to her.

One of the Hashmallim turned my way, although it was hard to tell if he was looking at me or not, since they didn't have actual faces. Not with the long cowls and robes that flowed over them, keeping them to a large, vaguely human shape that seemed to suck in all the light and joy and happiness around them and leave the air filled with fear, horror, and pretty much outright unending terror.

The Hashmallim suddenly reared back; then the long, robe-covered arms rose and seemed to cover his head before he spun around and oozed his way up the stairs at a fairly fast clip.

"Oh yeah, I remember you," I called after him. "Want some more of my hump, my hump, my lovely lady lumps?"

"What on earth?" Mabel asked, incredulous.

I looked back again and waggled my eyebrows at her. "'My Humps' by Black Eyed Peas. It got me out of the Akasha the time I was stuck here by a bad Guardian. Had to sing it nonstop for three days before he threw me out. Guess he remembers me!"

The other Hashmallim weren't so affected, and after standing like a row of intensely scary robe-covered statues apparently made out of the stuff that is in a black hole, one of them lifted an arm and pointed it at Parisi. "You are no longer Sovereign," he said in a voice that sounded like two granite slabs grinding together.

"I am a warrior of the blood," she repeated. "Stand aside, or you will be destroyed."

Behind her, Finch and Hunter exchanged glances; then both hefted their weapons and stepped forward next to us.

"Leave," the chatty one said. "Now."

"Excellent. You want to do this the hard way," she answered, and rolled her shoulders again before lifting her sword.

"I don't know that I'd do what you're thinking of doing—" Sally started to say, but Parisi evidently wasn't going to wait around to see what the Hashmallim would do.

She was on the first one in the time between heartbeats, slashing and cutting and twirling around him in a dance that was simultaneously beautiful and starkly horrible.

Finch yelled something in French and jumped forward to another Hashmallim, while Hunter, with a profane oath under his breath, shifted into a smoky-colored dragon and roared so loudly as he attacked, the echoes seemed to go on forever.

I joined in the fun as much as I could, although it turns out that the Hashmallim's bodies were oddly intangible. Every time I thought I was clamping down on a calf or thigh, the form seemed to melt away in my mouth.

That's when the other three Hashmallim showed up and immediately jumped into the fray. Things went chaotic then, with dark power being splashed all over the place by the Hashmallim, sending both me and Finch flying across the room to slam into one of the stone walls. Little corgi-shaped stars danced before my eyes for a few seconds before I heard a high, feminine scream, and suddenly, I was on my feet, racing across the room to where four of the Hashmallim had ganged up on Parisi.

Hunter and Finch, now back-to-back, were attacking the other two while trying to stay out of the way of the spells and dark power that was thrown at them.

Parisi screamed again as she went down under a massive black mound that was the Hashmallim pig-piling on her.

"Nooo!" I yelled, but when I was halfway across the room, a black shape emerged from the water and, before I could blink, it was throwing Hashmallim off my mom.

It was Desi, and he apparently had no trouble dealing with the Hashmallim, because he seemed to twist their forms until they dissolved into nothing, their long black robes drifting to the ground.

Parisi rose, blood dripping from a scratch on her cheek. For a moment she and Desi stared at each other; then he reached out and gently touched the blood on her face, saying something in a language that sounded really old.

"Get them out of here," I heard Sally tell Mabel. "As soon as the last Hashmallim is sent back to the Court, take them to Aisling's house."

"Is that what happens to them when they're destroyed?" Mabel asked, her eyes huge as she watched Finch and Hunter fight.

"Yes. Get ready," Sally answered, and I could feel her pulling in power around herself.

"All right, but it has to be their wish," Mabel warned.

Evidently Desi realized there were still two Hashmallim, now caught in battle with Hunter and Finch, and he left Parisi to fling himself on the gaolers.

It was over in less than a minute. I stood panting and still spitting out the taste of boggart blood when Mabel hustled forward. "Right, now is the time we leave. Parisi, I can take you and Desislav to Aisling's house. Sound good? Desislav, you agree? Awesome! Off we go."

She didn't really give them time to agree—she just grabbed Parisi's arm with one hand, and Desi's with the other, and boom! They were gone.

"And now you two," Sally said, her hands dancing as she spoke the words of banishment, sending Hunter and me to the Akasha.

I don't know how long we were there, but it was enough time for me to go to the nearest vending machine and see if they had anything good to nom. They didn't, because it was a place of punishment, so the whole thing was filled with Raisinets, Necco Wafers, and Circus Peanuts. "And ain't no one gonna eat those," I told Hunter.

He looked like he was about to answer, but blipped out of the Akasha. A few seconds later, Aisling summoned me, too.

"—and I don't know why you're making such a big deal about it," she was saying to an obviously furious Drake. He stood glaring at her with smoke curling out of his nose. "It was nothing. Absolutely nothing."

"What did I miss?" I asked, glancing around.

Parisi and Desi were standing next to the big window that looked out on the square, but were looking at each other instead of the pretty park where I had my walkies.

"Nothing. Absolutely nothing," Aisling repeated, squeezing Drake's arm before she kissed the tip of his nose. "Hunter winked at me before he left, that's all."

"Another dragon winked at my mate," Drake said, sounding outraged. "A master of an ouroboros tribe winked at you. Why did he do so? He must want to steal you!"

"Oh, for the love of Pete ... Drake, it was a wink. He doesn't want me. I have three kids and a sexy-as-sin dragon of my own—no one else is going to want me."

"Why. Did. He. Wink?" Drake asked through gritted teeth.

"Jealous much?" I couldn't help but ask, still keeping an eye on my parents. Sally, who had been standing at the far end of the room speaking softly on her phone, turned around to smile at us all.

"I'm happy to say that all the Hashmallim are accounted for, and have been given new physical forms and returned to their duties protecting the Akasha. Are we all done here?"

"Why aren't you listening to me?" Aisling asked Drake. "Why do you think I'd lie?"

"I don't think anything so heinous. You are my mate, and you are madly in love with me. I trust you with everything I have, but the same does not apply to masters of ouroboros tribes who can challenge me for you and attempt to steal you from me and our children."

Aisling is made of nicer stuff than me, because where I thought Drake was being overbearing and ridiculous, she just smiled and leaned in to him to whisper, "You know full well I would never let that happen again. You're mine, and I'm keeping you, so get over your wyvern jealousy when it concerns unmated male dragons, and tell me how much you missed me while you were in Hungary."

He kissed her, murmured something that sounded a lot like a brief apology and reassurance that he couldn't live without her; then he turned to Sally and asked, "Why did he wink?"

"Hmm?" She looked up from her phone before tucking it away. "Oh, that would be the blood bond. Aisling had to have some sort of a bond with Hunter in order to be able to summon him from the Akasha, and since she refused to kiss him for an exchange that way, they pricked their fingers and mingled blood. A blood bond is always best, I find."

"You don't have one with me," I told her while Drake roared, outright roared, and Aisling had to take him to the other end of the room and have yet another round of reassuring the jealous dragon.

Sally gave me a curious look that melted into a tiny smile, one I felt was meant just for me. "But you are special."

"Amen to that, sister," I said, giving her a quick sniffle and head rub on her leg. "And speaking of that, thanks muchly."

She glanced to where Parisi and Desi were speaking quietly, her smile fading. "I wish that I could be certain you will continue to be grateful for the actions we've taken today."

It was an odd sort of thing to say, and I was about to ask her more, but Aisling's phone started dinging with an alarm for an upcoming video call, and Sally used that as an excuse to leave.

"I'm willing to let it go for now, but I warn you that the next occasion we have dragon-fighting time, Hunter is going to be present," Drake said in a tone filled with portent. "I have a few things to work out with him."

"Yes, yes, you can beat the tar out of each other the next time you boys have a shindig. Sally, we can't thank you enough for everything you've done. I'm sure Christian and Allie share my gratitude." While Aisling and Drake saw Sally to the door, I wandered over to my parents.

"You came to rescue me? To save me?" Desi was asking when I stopped next to them.

"Of course." Parisi gave a little shrug. "It was my duty as a defender. You said we know each other? I have no recollection of you, and yet …"

"Heya," I told Desi when he turned to frown at me interrupting their tête-à-tête. "So, it turns out you're my dad."

He blinked a couple of times, his expression filled with incredulity. "I did not sire a dog!"

I tipped my head to the side because Ash told me it made me look adorable. "Yeah, that's just my preferred form. Ever since I became a demon."

"You what?" he all but yelled, glancing again at Parisi. "Is this true? Our child became a demon? After everything I did to protect him, he became a demon?"

"I don't know," she said, lifting her hands in an obvious gesture of confusion. "I don't have a child, let alone a dog. I live by myself, although I do have two beehives. I like the bees."

"He says he's our son," Desi said, pointing at me.

"He's rather confused, I think," she answered.

"Maybe this'll help," I said, and shifted into human form.

Desi stared at me, his eyes first widening, then narrowing until they were slits of glittering black. "Effrijim?"

"That's the name, although I go by Jim now. Not that I want to complain, but the full name is a bit girly."

"I just hope you can move past the whole thing with Hunter—Jim, what the hell?" Aisling stopped midway across the room.

"Abaddon," Desi and I said at the same time.

"Why is it naked aga—"Drake stopped in mid-complaint and looked between Desi and me. "Well, that answers the question of whether or not Jim is really their child."

"You look just like your dad," Aisling said, coming forward to whip a throw off a couch and toss it at me.

I wrapped it around my waist. She looked first at Desi, then at me. "Right down to the same hairline, and eye color. Although Desi doesn't have a cleft chin."

We all looked at Parisi, who looked unperturbed at the fact that her chin *did* have a slight cleft.

"Effrijim?" my dad asked again, leaning close to me as he searched my face. It was a bit uncomfy, because he was definitely exuding little tendrils of dark power, but I figured this was the best way for my parents to see who I was, so I stood there and let them stare. Then he hugged me, a full body hug, the sort that makes you feel like you're wrapped in soft, warm cotton. It was a hug that reassured, a hug that said the things that words couldn't say. I hugged him back, a bit moist of eye, because how often does a demon get to meet his parents?

"But … this dog form …" Desi stopped, and took a step back from me.

"Jim loves being a Newfie," Aisling said, leaning against Drake, their arms around each other in a way that made me feel a bit better. Not that I cared much about their tiffs, but seeing my parents was doing a number on my emotions, and things were always easier if Drake wasn't being unreasonable about Aisling. "It's the form it always chooses, and I have to admit, as dogs go, it's pretty handsome. Not that it's not very handsome as a man, but we are all happy with it being a dog. I hope that doesn't upset you. I've given it permission to change its form at will, so if it does, I'm sure Jim will be happy to go into human form around you. Clothed human form." The last bit was added with a side-eye at me.

"Yeah, but dog form is so much better," I said, then, figuring the parents had had enough time to come to grips with me, shifted back into my fabulous form, all floofy black fur, dashing white spot on my chest and some toes, and a truly magnificent tail. "So, Aisling is my demon lord, and I live with her and Drake and the spawn, but we should probably talk about visitation rights."

Aisling's laptop burbled to life before anyone could answer, and she moved over to flip it around.

"We're going to have a meeting," I told the parents, who were still at the window. I nosed Parisi until she sat on the love seat, Desi reluctantly joining her.

"We have much to talk about. How you found me, why you came after me, and what we're going to do in order to protect you and Effrijim," he told Parisi.

"Just Jim," I reminded him. "Protect us from what?"

"Are we early? I'm sorry if we are, but Christian was anxious to get things rolling." Allie and Christian came into view on the video screen, joined almost immediately by a window that featured Brom, looking mildly uncomfortable.

"Hi," he said when Aisling greeted him. "Sullivan is chasing Anduin. He's naked because he escaped his bath. Baltic is talking to the First Dragon. He's pissed about one of Baltic's brothers. Heya, Jim."

"Heya," I said in return, then tipped my head toward the love seat. "Got my parents here."

"Cool," he said, obviously studying them.

"It's a pleasure to meet you both," Allie said, and Christian added a more formal greeting.

"My Beloved and I are grateful for your help, and are desirous of assisting both of you in whatever ways you need," he said with a nod of his head. "Should you seek aid in finding lodging, income, etc., we will be happy to do whatever is needed."

"It goes without saying that we're here to help, as well," Aisling said, sitting on the arm of Drake's chair.

"We have more than enough room if you'd like to stay a few days while we're tackling the subject of the thane."

"Thane?" Desi asked.

"It's something the Dark Ones need help with," Parisi told him. "He's a very bad person, and they are worried that he will wreak vengeance through the mortal world."

"Perhaps if we give them the whole story?" Aisling said, sitting back as Ysolde replaced Brom on the screen. "Christian can explain it much better than I can."

I watched my parents while Christian and Allie explained the whole thing with the bad vampire ancestor.

Parisi looked interested, but she kept sending quick looks toward Desi. I couldn't tell if she was ogling him, or trying to figure out who he was.

Honestly, I think it was a bit of both. He definitely was returning her interest with glances that came close to a dragon's smolder, alternating with odd little looks cast my way.

Aisling had warned me before we started the expedition that they might be a bit put off by me being in dog form, so I decided Desi needed a bit more time before he could swing into the dad role. Since he'd been without us for sixteen hundred years, I reckoned it might take a couple of days to become comfortable with my magnificent form.

"Thane," Desi repeated slowly.

"Do you know him?" Parisi asked.

"No." He frowned at my toes. "Yes. Perhaps. I have a vague memory of four thanes who tried to interfere with Abaddon, but they were dealt with. Parisi ensured the Court handled them."

"I don't think so," Parisi said, shaking her head, although I noticed that her hand had slid over to rest on his leg. "There must be another Parisi, one who did all these things. I am just a simple Defender of the Blood."

"I don't think you're a simple anything," I said, looking at my mom. She still had the Sovereign mark on her forehead, and the way she'd dealt with the boggarts and Hashmallim said a lot.

"Thank you. I think." She lifted a hand like she was going to pat my head, but pulled back before doing so.

"It's OK. You can pet me. I especially like belly scritches," I told her, and moved over to sit between them, leaning on her as I rested my head on her leg.

Aisling sniffled, and accepted the handkerchief that Drake pulled from his pocket.

"Oh. Well, I do like animals ..." Parisi gave my head a couple of pats. I enjoyed watching her expression change from hesitation to embarrassment to a sort of grudging pleasure as she gave my ears a quick pat.

I turned to find Desi watching me with an indescribable look. "You really prefer this form?" he asked.

"Yeah. You upset?" I turned so I could look at him better.

He was silent for a moment, then shook his head. "When I was a child, I fancied being a horse, so it makes sense. Very well. You're a demon dog. You live with the dragon?"

"That's right, we haven't done formal introductions," Aisling said, and quickly went through them, including Ysolde, Christian, and Allie. "As Jim said, I'm technically its demon lord, but it is a much loved member of our family."

Drake made a noise that resembled a stifled snort, but kept his face placid when Ash shot him a look.

"I see." Desi turned to Parisi. "Are you happy with this situation?"

"Why wouldn't I be?" she asked in return.

Allie had evidently had enough of our family time, because she said, "Can you help us putting this missing thane back in the Hour that holds him? Our nephew is lord of the Hour, but of course, he can't leave it to help with the Thrall-wrangling."

Desi shook his head. "If the thane you refer to is one of the foursome I remember, then there would be no problem in returning him to the Hour. That is, assuming I had my blood moon, but I no longer possess it."

"What's a blood moon when it's at home?" I asked for Aisling, because I could see she was dying to ask it.

"My relic," Desi said, his gaze on Parisi's face. She looked mildly confused again, but somehow focused at the same time, as if she was trying hard to pin down her memories. At least, that's what I assumed she was doing. "It was destroyed when Effrijim was born. Without it, my powers are limited."

"You are still a demigod," Christian said, his voice velvety and smooth, but there was a hardness in it that was kind of normal with vamps.

"I am, but one with limited powers," Desi repeated. "Once the blood moon was destroyed, I was left depleted."

"I don't wish to be argumentative," Christian said, "but even a demigod who lost his relic should have had enough power to escape the imprisonment."

"Of course I could," Desi said without so much as batting an eye.

"You could?" Parisi asked, her hand now in his, both resting on his leg. "Then why didn't you leave?"

"Because I accepted the terms of my banishment," he said in that same matter-of-fact tone. He had a bit of an Eastern European accent, but for the most part, he spoke English well.

"How come you speak English?" I asked. "Aren't you from somewhere in the Balkans? That's what Sally told me."

For a moment, amusement flashed across his face, and he held up one arm. A big watch was on his wrist. "The boggarts. The last few years they all started sporting waterproof smart watches. Whenever they'd get close enough for me to grab them, I'd throttle them and take their watches and use them until they ran out; then I'd wait for the next boggart to swim past. Learning about the modern world helped pass the time."

"Wow," Ysolde said, and I noticed that she was now joined by Baltic. He wore his usual inscrutable expression. "That's amazing that you did all that. I'm sorry if we were late and missed the explanation, but why did you allow yourself to be banished in such an appalling place?"

"Parisi was dying." He looked at her, and for a moment, there was so much pain in his eyes that both my mom and I leaned into him. "She had childbed fever. The bleeding wouldn't stop after the babe was born. The only way to save her was to send her to the Beyond, where she would survive."

"I'm not who you think I am, but I am so sorry that happened to you," Parisi told him, giving him—and in the process me, because I was still between them—a hug. "How very tragic that you should lose your wife to childbirth."

He touched her cheek. "It was worth any sacrifice to know you and Effrijim were safe. I didn't expect you to come after me, however." His jaw tightened. "And now we must decide what to do to keep you safe again.

The reaper could take you back to the Beyond, and as for Effrijim …"

"Why does Parisi need to be kept safe?" Ysolde asked.

Aisling pointed to her image on the laptop. "What Ysolde said. And who is the threat to Parisi? As for Jim, I can't think of anyone other than some imp clans that would like to harm it."

"The threat is Abaddon, of course," Desi answered. "The terms of our agreement were that I would accept banishment to the Thirteenth Hour, and no harm would befall my son." He turned to look at me. "What I don't understand is how you became a demon. Parisi's woman swore she would see the Court protected you."

"They did," I answered, then scrunched up my face as I wondered whether I should tell them what happened before I met Aisling. I decided it didn't really reflect me in a good way, so I'd tell them later, once they appreciated just how fantabulous was my form choice. "And if you're talking about Mags, she was there for a long time, and got me into the sprite cadre. Then she moved on to the Beyond, and a few other Sovereigns rolled through, and the last time I saw Hildegarde, she told me that my future lay outside of the Court, so I headed out and ended up hanging around Abaddon for a few hundred years."

"Hildegarde," Parisi said on kind of a snort. "She was naught but a …" She stopped and frowned, then looked puzzled. "She was … who was this person? Why do I know her, but don't?"

"It was the spell I cast upon you as you entered the Beyond," Desi told her, wrapping an arm around her and pulling her close to him.

"You bespelled me?" she asked, suddenly bristling with anger and, to my surprise, also armed with a wickedly sharp dagger, which she held to Desi's throat. "I do not take kindly to people casting spells upon me!"

"My love, my stars, my moon," he said, shaking his head as he moved her hand so he could kiss her. "I could not ask for a better sign that your memories can be restored."

"Dude," I said, eyeing the dagger. "Being upside down for sixteen hundred years has done a number on your reason, 'cause it just ain't normal for someone who loves you to pull a knife on you."

"You don't know Parisi as I do," he said, smiling at her.

She smiled back and, with a move so fast I almost missed it, stuck the dagger back into the side of her boot. "Perhaps you do know me, after all," she told him, and probably would have gone in for another kiss, but at that moment, Ysolde spoke.

"I'm so sorry, I hate to be the one hurrying people along, especially those who are long-lost and somewhat amnesiac due to mind wipes, but it's date night tonight, and Baltic says he's taking me to a nursery so I can browse amongst the plants."

"That's a date?" Allie asked, then apologized. "Sorry, I don't mean to harsh your date-night mellow."

"Ysolde loves plants," was all that Baltic said, but the look they exchanged was unmistakable.

"I think maybe it would help zip things along if we updated Parisi and Desi about the current state of Abaddon," Aisling said. "There's been a big turnover the last twenty or so years. More recently, Bael has been trapped in the Duat, the Egyptian underworld, ruled over by his uncle. Asmodeus was killed by Bael before he went to the Duat, and a couple of the other demon lords got kicked out, banished to the Akasha, or outright killed."

Desi's head snapped around at the mention of Bael. "He is gone? You are certain?"

"Which one?" Aisling asked him. "Bael?"

"Yes. He long sought the blood moon. I can't believe he could be confined with it in his possession. That should not be possible."

"That's because he doesn't have it. Or rather, he didn't have it when he went to the Duat," Aisling said, glancing at Drake.

"Sally could explain the actual events, as she was involved with part of it," Drake said, one finger rubbing his chin as he looked into the distance. "But as I recall, she said the Tools of Bael had their origin in a powerful relic. I don't believe she named it, but if you say Bael had a hand in your banishment, then it makes sense that your relic was used in the creation of his three Tools."

"Where are these Tools?" Desi asked, leaping to his feet as if he was going to rush right out to claim them.

"Destroyed," Aisling said. "They are no more. Drake used to have all three, but in a story that's way too long to tell now, they went into Asmodeus's custody for a bit, then were destroyed with Sally's help."

"Destroyed?" Desi sat down again, his face stark. I wanted to say something, but remembered Aisling telling me to take it easy on my parents for a bit while they got used to being reunited with me, so instead I just sniffed his knees in a supportive manner.

He absently patted me on the head. He gave nice pats.

"Let me be sure I understand this situation." Parisi, who had been looking sympathetically at Desi, pinned

Aisling back with a hard look. "You're saying that this Bael person responsible for sending Desi to the Thirteenth Hour is no longer a threat to him?"

"He never was a threat to me, not so long as I held the blood moon," Desi said, his brows pulling together into a line.

"And someone," Parisi continued, "one of you dragons or Dark Ones, said that the Court had domain over this Hour."

"That's what we were told by Finch and Sally," Christian answered. He, also, was frowning.

I looked over at Drake. Frown. Baltic—frown. I decided that was the look of the day, and furrowed my own brow, wondering what Desi would do once he realized what Parisi was chasing.

"I pointed out that Asmodeus, who was the second-most powerful demon lord next to Bael, was killed, and there's a new lot of demon lords running Abaddon," Aisling reminded him.

I saw the moment the penny dropped for Desi. He stood up slowly, his hands first flexing, then curled into fists. "The blood moon was destroyed, in whatever form it was. Bael was banished. The other two princes who founded Abaddon with me are long dead. In short, anyone who posed a threat to Parisi and Effrijim are no more."

"Uh-oh," I said under my breath. I think Parisi heard me, but she didn't pay any attention when I got up and moved over to sit on Aisling's feet, leaning back on her.

"Jim," she whispered, and tried to push me off. "Move!"

Drake looked at me, then at Desi, who had turned when Parisi got to her feet and put a hand on his arm.

Drake, too, got up. Aisling shot him a startled look, but his attention was focused on Desi.

"OK, that's cool, in a bad sort of way," I said softly when power began to emit from Desi. It was like his whole body was lit up with a weird blackness that was both glowing and yet as dark as ink, and exuded a coldness that made me lean back harder against Aisling's legs. Drake took a step forward, his eyes narrowed.

"Why," Desi said, and had to stop for a moment, obviously struggling to control the power that crawled all over him. "Why, if the Court was responsible for maintaining the imprisonment during the reign of Bael, Hath, and the others, did no one release me when they were no longer a threat?"

"That is a very good question," Parisi said, looking pointedly at Aisling.

Drake moved in front, effectively blocking their view of Ash and me. "Aisling is not responsible for any of the regrettable actions that led to your imprisonment. Quite the opposite in that she has worked a good deal to ensure your freedom."

"That's true, she did," Parisi told Desi, and murmured an apology at Aisling, who was holding my collar as she peered around Drake's butt to where the others stood.

"I see why he's upset," Ysolde told Baltic. "That really is evil that no one at the Court thought to let him out."

He said nothing, just watched the screen with his usual expression of knowing something the rest of us don't.

"I believe we're slightly off track, conversationally speaking," Allie said. "As horrible as it is that you weren't released earlier, the fact remains that we still need help with the thane. I'm sure you'll want a few days to get adjusted to the mortal world, but—"

"Who do I owe for my release?" Desi asked Parisi, gesturing toward us. "The dragons?"

"Somewhat, yes. They arranged for the reaper and Sally, along with the Dark Ones," she answered.

A muscle worked in his jaw; then his hands relaxed. "I will not repay kindness with sorrow. Come, Parisi. There is much we must do."

"Wait, you can't just leave!" Ysolde said at the same time that Allie and Christian also voiced protests. "The vamps need you."

"The Thrall can wait," Desi said, taking Parisi's hand and more or less storming across the room to the doors. "There is something I must attend to first."

"What?" Aisling asked, having finally shoved me off her feet so she could stand next to Drake. "If you knew how much trouble this thane could cause—"

Desi stopped at the door and looked back. I took the moment to nose the laptop around so it was now facing them. "The Court must pay for their actions."

"Holy crack on rye," I said with a low whistle. I mean, on one hand I was super impressed with how cool my dad was, what with the dark glowy power now snapping and crackling around him like he was one of those electricity globe things, but on the other hand, I had an idea where he was headed, and it wasn't going to be good.

Not for anyone.

"You're not serious, are you?" Ysolde asked. "You can't be seriously thinking to make the Court pay?"

Desi looked at Parisi, who met his gaze before turning to look at Aisling, Drake, and me. Then she nodded, and took his hand. "Yes, I will help you. I have sworn to protect those who need my aid. You have been done wrong by the people who have also sworn to protect, and for that, they must pay. For you, and only you, will I risk Don Diego taking over my Pilates class."

"Holy shit," Aisling whispered to Drake. "Is she saying what I think she's saying? The Don Diego thing aside, because I don't understand that at all. Who knew they had Pilates in the Beyond?"

Desi turned to look at the computer. "Dark One, you have my oath I will assist you with the thane in acknowledgment of the debt I owe you and the dragons, but that will only happen after I have wrought vengeance upon those who were responsible for keeping me imprisoned when I should have been released. Effrijim, I recognize you as my son. You will join us in our war."

"Er ... " I said, pursing my lips before saying, "Yeah, about that ... I'm more a lover than a fighter, really. Have I told you about my girlfriend, Cecile? She's an adorable, if cranky, Welsh corgi, and—"

"Where will we go?" Parisi asked Desi. "I have no home in the mortal world."

"We will find a place. We will need many provisions for the war," he told her.

"Jim, I don't want you thinking I'm telling you what to do, because despite being your demon lord, I never want to act like one, but I'm not terribly comfortable with the idea of you joining your parents at this time." Aisling's eyes were worried as she rubbed one of my ears. "I do understand that they're your family, though, so if you wanted to stay with them ..." She stopped and cleared her throat.

I answered her in the same near whisper she'd used. "They're fun and all ... well, interesting, maybe, more than fun, because that aura my dad is exuding is unlike anything I've ever seen in Abaddon, and yes, they are my mom and dad, but I don't really know them. Besides, you're also my family, and you'd be up a creek without a paddle if you didn't have me."

"Dammit, Jim, don't make me cry in front of powerful demigods and their equally powerful Sovereign mates," she said, but gave me a quick hug to let me know she cared.

I rubbed my head on her leg in return.

"Effrijim?" Desi stopped speaking in low tones with Parisi and pinned me back with a look that had me sitting up straighter. "Do you join us in our war?"

"Like, can I help from the sidelines?" I asked, worried that I was going to lose parents I'd just found, but at the same time, I couldn't just bail. "Not that I have a particular beef with the Court, since I was treated well when I was there, but I can't really leave Aisling now. She has Guardian stuff she needs me for, and the spawn like to have me tell them about history and things like that, and then there's Cecile. We're working on a way to make her immortal, because dogs do not live long enough, and I can't really help Amelie—that's Cecile's mom—find a dog immortality spell if I'm busy fighting a holy war."

"Very well," Desi said, giving me a little nod. "If it is your wish to remain with the dragons, then I will honor that desire. Know that you will always have a home with us, but so long as you are not kept from us, we will agree to your terms. Once your mother and I are settled, we will contact you. As for your contribution to the war … if it would make life with your dragons difficult, we will simply have to rely upon your sister, instead. A triumvirate is always stronger. Parisi?"

She cracked her knuckles. "Let's go find a domicile so that we may make plans. My sword itches for blood of the Court."

Protests emerged from the computer, with Ysolde saying again that he couldn't just walk off, but that's exactly what he did.

One moment they were there at the door, and the next, they were gone, and the sound of the front door closing drifted in to us.

Drake looked at Aisling. She stared first at him, then moved her gaze to me.

I blinked at her.

"Sister?" she asked.

"Yeah, that threw me, too. Fires of Abaddon, Aisling ... I have a whole entire family I didn't know about!" I got up, shook, and toyed with the idea of going to my room. I suddenly had a desire to tell Cecile about the happenings, which meant I had to have Amelie put me on speakerphone on her end.

"What about us?" Allie asked, her voice rising. For a moment, I'd forgotten they were still on the call. "What about the thane?"

Christian looked mad enough to spit, but rather than saying anything about my parents, he simply said, "We appreciate all the time and help you have given us. Since I'm sure you will refuse monetary remuneration, please text us with the name of a charity you support, and we will offer them a donation in lieu of that."

"Keep in touch," Allie said before Christian ended their call.

"This took a turn I absolutely did not expect," Ysolde said. "What are we going to do now? Should we warn Sally, or the Sasha person who's running the Court now? We can't leave the vamps out in the cold."

"No, of course not," Aisling said.

"It is not our battle to fight," Drake reminded her.

"Perhaps not, but that doesn't mean we can't help allies," she answered.

"Dark Ones are no allies of dragonkin," Baltic said.

"They're not really enemies, though, are they?" Ysolde asked. "Besides, I like Allie. I just don't know what we should do about Desi and Parisi."

"Let's call the others, and see what the Mates and Friends group can come up with," Aisling suggested.

I left to go to my room where my cell phone was sitting next to the super-comfy dog bed Aisling had given me as a Christmas present.

ME

Did you know I had a sister?

SALLY

…

SALLY

Who mentioned her? What am I saying … it must be Desislav?

ME

Yeah. He said something about needing her.

SALLY

Oh, dear. I think … yes, I think it's time to bring Terrin in. If Desi is going to summon her, all hell is going to break out.

ME

It's when you say things like that I wonder about whether you should have been running Abaddon rather than the Court.

SALLY

You know me so well. Did they declare war?

ME

Yup.

SALLY

I assumed that's the way it was heading. Very well. Lines have been drawn. I will inform Terrin.

ME

What about the Court? That's who Desi said betrayed him.

SALLY

And who was Sovereign for the last two hundred years of his incarceration?

ME

Crapbeans.

SALLY

Exactly. Ah well. A demigod and his pissed-off warrior of a mate after my head will add a little spice to my life. That is, so long as they don't find your half sister. If they do that, all bets are off.

ME

My sister is a half sister? Is she Parisi's kid, or Desi's?

ME

Sally?

ME

Great. Not only is there a killer thane roaming around the mortal world, now my pissed-off demigod father with a chip on his shoulder, and scary-as-Abaddon mom with a deep love of lopping off beings' heads, are starting a war they can't win.

SALLY

Some days, it's just not worth chewing the leather straps off the straitjacket, is it?

CALL ME, MAYBE?

My lovely one! I hope you enjoyed MIDNIGHT IN THE GARDEN OF OKAY AND MEH, which I handcrafted from the finest artisanal words just for you. If you are new to my dragon books, and want to see more about Drake, Aisling, Jim, and all the other denizens of the Otherworld, feel free to dive into YOU SLAY ME, the first book in the Green Dragon series.

If you're *not* new to the dragons, or just want more fun stuff, head to my website to join my newsletter for exclusive reader bonuses like sneak peaks, extra scenes, shop discounts, and bonus epilogues.

It's free and fun. And full of weirdness. Admittedly, lots of weirdness…

ABOUT KATIE

Bird skeleton washer.

Doll's house salesperson to royalty.

King Tut tour guide.

Katie MacAlister has not just worked odd jobs, she's lived an even odder life. Luckily, she's always had a book with her to take her away from the weirdness.

Two years after she started writing novels, Katie sold her first romance, *Noble Intentions*. More than seventy books later, her novels have been translated into numerous languages, been recorded as audiobooks, received several awards, and have been regulars on the *New York Times*, *USA Today*, *Wall Street Journal*, and *Publishers Weekly* bestseller lists.

Katie is a widow who lives in the Pacific Northwest with two dogs, and can often be found lurking around online.

You are welcome to join Katie's official discussion group on Facebook, as well as connect on Instagram. For more information, visit www.katiemacalister.com